Long

MW00777504

A fireman with a wounded heart and a woman with an adventurous free spirit, can one choice change their lives?

A sought after internationally recognized photographer, Cassie Sinclair, is at a turning point after an accident on the side of a mountain. Now struggling with uncertainties, she returns home for her brother's wedding and an extended stay. When she is suddenly needed as a backup nanny for the handsome firefighter's daughter, her uncertainties multiply when sparks fly between them and the unexpected attraction throws them both into turmoil.

Hunter Claremont has been through enough heartache and disappointment where love is concerned. He's focused now on his new job as a fireman in Sunset Bay and raising his young daughter, helping her overcome the tragedy of losing her mother. They've found a place to start over in the small coastal town, among its caring and sometimes eccentric folks. And they've found friends in the Sinclairs, the family his sister has married into, with strong family ties and big hearts, who have welcomed him and his sweet daughter with open arms. His only problem...he keeps thinking about Cassie Sinclair and he can't seem to get her off his mind.

Can a small-town fireman and a woman with wanderlust in her veins find a happy ending?

LONGING FOR US

Sunset Bay Romance, Book Six

DEBRA CLOPTON

Longing for Us

Copyright © 2020 Debra Clopton Parks

CHAPTER ONE

Cassie Sinclair marveled at the beauty of the breezy December afternoon as friends and family gathered along the pier and surrounding area of the Sunset Bay Marina and watched as her brother Jonah and his sweet bride, Summer, recited their vows together. They'd met on this pier and loved the view and the atmosphere, and had decided this was the perfect place for them to have their wedding. Cassie had to agree.

They had invited anyone and everyone in the community who wanted to come. Jonah was like that, a wonderful, open and loving guy who everyone loved. It showed with the crowd who had gathered here today to celebrate with them. It was a festive and warm, casual wedding, and love for the couple abounded as their own love for each other hung in the air like crystals sparkling in the sunlight.

Looking at them through the lens of her camera, she snapped several shots and knew soon the light would be perfect for their photos. This was where her heart needed to be. These kinds of photos. She was usually suspended from something or hanging off something, or even swimming underwater, taking photos of people and their happily-ever-after bliss. Her photo shoots, from weddings to wildlife to landscapes—anything that needed a beautiful shot in an unusual and potentially amazing way of capturing life through a camera lens—provided such an adrenaline rush. Her love and her skill had taken her all over the world. She lived for it, loved it, and yet she loved taking pictures of her family in these happy moments of their lives.

Her brother looked so ecstatically happy as he

recited his vows, and Summer looked adoringly at him and with such love as he spoke of his love for her. And when it was her time, she was so full of love that it was breathtaking. Cassie snapped shot after shot for the perfect photo. She lived for that perfect shot where their love shined through their entire bodies as they gazed into each other's eyes like now, in this tranquil place with Jonah and Summer.

Cassie's insides quaked, flashing back to her last assignment a week earlier when she'd been suspended off the side of an Australian mountain's edge, capturing a shot of a rock-climbing bride and groom. They'd wanted to say their vows standing on a narrow ledge as the sun rose. It was unusual to have the shots at sunrise. So they were working with limited light until the first rays broke on the distant horizon. She had to be ready and suspended in the perfect spot for the shots. She'd scouted the rock face, and her crew had set everything up the day before so that she could be in place. She appreciated what the couple wanted; she was a skilled rock climber herself and had done similar shots many times. She was known for shots like this. In instances such as that moment taking the shots of the couple, her hands were busy holding the camera and she was reliant completely on her gear, cables, and the anchors holding her in place. She'd never had an anchor fail, until that moment. She was grateful her safety measures were in place and held, and she landed on a small ledge below her without more than a sore body from the impact of hitting the wall then the ledge and the scrapes that came with it.

It had only been because she was tied off to her other anchor that she lived. But in those moments of falling, of grappling for control, her life flashed before her. Just as she'd always heard, she realized in that brief flash that there was so much in her life that she hadn't fulfilled. That instance was the closest she'd ever come to death, as far as she was aware, and yes, her regrets had been what flashed through her mind. These moments that she captured of everyone's love, even those of the couple she'd just taken before falling, were safe because the camera was still fastened to her when she landed on the ledge. Those expressions of her recent couple were safe. But in those seconds, her main regret was that she was never going to have a man look at her like all of her grooms had done to their brides. No, sadly, she was going to go down in history as the photographer who fell to her death taking photographs of someone else's love story.

When she'd hit the ledge and lived, it had appeared that she was calm and collected as she'd gotten up, given a thumbs-up, and then been extracted from the ledge. She'd put on a brave face and handed her camera to her assistant. It was the week of Christmas and she'd missed the family Christmas to prepare for this wedding, but she had made certain she would be finished so she could be off for Jonah and Summer's wedding the week after Christmas. But after the accident, she'd extended her time off for a month. It was the first time she would be home for a month in a very long time.

And for the moment she wasn't sure, but she might extend it. She was thankful to be home and no one knew the extent of the trauma that she suffered internally from the fall. From realizing that her life might not be as great and perfect as everyone believed.

She'd been interviewed by several magazines over the years about the world-class, exciting life she lived. About her adventurous spirit and compared to the likes of her brother Tate, who was also famous in his own right for the lifestyle he'd carved out for himself on the other side of the lens. But recently Tate—even Tate—had found love and a new satisfaction for having his home base here in their hometown of Sunset Bay.

Her camera automatically went to Tate, who stood beside Jonah. His loving gaze was locked on his bride, Gigi, who was one of the bridesmaids. Cassie had been asked to be a bridesmaid too but as always, she'd declined so that she could take the photos. She was very seldom in the actual wedding shots of her family during the wedding. Afterward she would get in the shots but not during the ceremony. She wanted to capture those moments, that beauty; it was her gift to them. She had her assistants take care of much of the receptions but the wedding photos were her baby.

As she focused back on Tate, her camera shifted and had found Summer's brother, Hunter. He stood beside Tate and was flanked by her other brothers,

Adam and Brad. He was a very fit and handsome fireman. He had recently moved to town to join the Sunset Bay Fire Department, of which her brother Brad was the fire chief. She knew that he was widowed and had an adorable little girl, Polly. Summer had moved to town with them to help care for her niece. They had a traumatic past surrounding the loss of his wife and the move, as far as she understood, was to help give Polly a new start and to help her overcome the tragedy.

The man had amazing eyes. She'd met him on her last trip in and had been instantly attracted to him. She'd shut that attraction down quickly, having absolutely no desire or intention of ever being drawn to settle down in the quaint little beach town she'd grown up in. Dating anyone in Sunset Bay was out of the question. One never knew what a date could lead to, and she was taking no chances. No, if she chose to settle down, she would settle somewhere exciting...maybe even overseas...but that was before the accident a week ago. Now she was questioning everything about her life. She knew this was her reaction to a traumatic experience. It would pass. She had life goals. And one bump in the road shouldn't shake her up, nor would she let it alter her life path.

Her gaze focused, and she startled as she realized his gaze was locked onto hers through the lens. He studied her calmly, knowing she was watching him through the camera. He didn't look away, didn't smile, didn't act self-conscious. He just stared back with those shadowed green eyes of his, framed by impossibly dark lashes, and held her gaze though he couldn't see her eyes. He held her captive in that moment. Something bubbled up inside her chest. Seconds ticked by and then she forced herself to react and move the camera back to the couple, where it should be, as the preacher told Jonah he could kiss his bride. She'd almost missed the shot.

The very idea that she'd been transfixed by Hunter Claremont and nearly missed one of her most important shots shook her.

She snapped the shot. Now was not the time to let a momentary attraction put any kind of a stumbling block in her future's path. She had enough to deal with in that she had the sudden longings for what her brothers and sister had found. She couldn't let her emotional reaction to her near-death experience push her in a direction that was all wrong for her.

She had to keep her wits about her, relax while she was here and then go back to the life she'd always, always wanted. And had worked and sacrificed to achieve.

* * *

Hunter Claremont felt a kick in the gut when he realized that the beautiful Cassie Sinclair's camera was aimed at him. He stared into the lens, unmoving, as his sister said her wedding vows to Jonah. He couldn't see Cassie's eyes but had realized the camera had been trained on him for seconds, even moments. Cassie was a beautiful, adventurous free spirit and he had tried to stay clear of her ever since he'd moved to town. Not too hard to do considering she was in town very little. She traveled all over the world with her cameras, and just dropped by to see her family when she could. She had a very strong grip on her future and her life.

He was just working hard as a fireman to get a new life, maintain it, and make it better for his daughter, Polly, after the horrific tragedy they'd suffered. He was still reeling from his wife's sudden and shocking declaration the night before the accident and the events that led up to the boat crash that killed her and almost killed Polly, too. He worried about Polly, and all he was doing right now in this small town was concentrating on getting his life straight with a new job, a new community, and a new start for her.

The attraction burning hot in his gut for the woman behind the camera was not something he was the least bit interested in. He had long ago realized that attraction meant nothing in the big picture of his life. He was not self-centered enough to pick his needs or his loneliness over what was best for his child. And right now, the simple attraction to a woman who stared at him from behind a camera was not important. Getting Polly back into a stable, happy situation was the only thing that mattered.

He realized that Cassie had turned the camera

elsewhere and a sense of both relief and disappointment washed through him. He switched his gaze to the preacher as he told Jonah he could kiss his bride.

He was so happy for his sweet sister, Summer, and thankful that she had found Jonah, the love of her life. It helped relieve some of the guilt he felt for having needed her so much to come help him with Polly, as his job as a fireman required him to work two- and three-day shifts, making it a necessity to have child care day and night. She was marrying into a wonderful family. The Sinclairs had welcomed Polly and him into their lives, and had made his daughter feel loved and that she belonged. It was what he'd prayed for and hoped for. He was forever grateful to this large family.

He smiled as Jonah and Summer finally stopped kissing and waved at the crowd.

"I thought they were never going to stop kissing." Brad laughed beside him.

"They can kiss as long as they want if it will keep that brilliant smile on my sister's face. Wow, she looks so happy."

"Now it's your turn," Brad said.

Brad was his boss and he knew more about Hunter's past than anyone. "You know I'm all about Polly right now." He was completely focused on making sure his daughter was healthy and emotionally cared for after losing her mother. Besides that, he'd been completely blindsided by his wife's betrayal, having learned about it right before her death. He had his own emotional baggage he was dealing with.

Nope, he was here to celebrate his sister's wedding, but he planned to never travel that road to heartache again.

CHAPTER TWO

"Hunter, you good-looking devil you," Lila Peabody cooed as she sidled up next to him. "Why are you hiding over here by the punch?"

He'd been standing next to the punch bowl, sipping on the pink, frothy punch they were serving with the cake at the wedding reception. He was trying to appear as if he were enjoying himself but the reality was that he wasn't. Polly was, though, and that made him happy. His sweet daughter was out on the dance floor, dancing with Summer and Jonah. The joy on her face sent a warm shaft of joy through him. Didn't make him want to go out there, though. He'd found himself searching out Cassie Sinclair a few times and that wasn't a good thing. Now he looked at Lila, his mind sifting through a barrage of warning signals as the sweet, mild-mannered-looking woman smiled sweetly at him with a twinkle in her blue eyes. She was pretty active on the matchmaking scene, and he had been avoiding her at all cost.

"Ms. Lila, how are you doing? It's a nice wedding, don't you think?"

She picked up a glass of punch and sipped as she studied him with speculation. "You should be out there dancing."

He pretended nonchalance. "I'm not much on dancing."

"I know, I know, you lost your wife, and I am so sorry about that. But it's been several years and you just have to get back on that horse and start riding it again. You're a young man and you just have to get back out there. I'm sure your sweet wife wouldn't want you mourning her forever."

He knew for a fact she wouldn't care one way or

the other. "I'm not interested—"

"Now, now, don't say that. You've got your whole life ahead of you, and you've got to think about that darling baby girl of yours. She's going to need a good woman to step in and love her, not replace her mama, but love her like her own—like her mama would have loved her if she were here."

He frowned, his brows crunching downward of their own accord at the realization that Lila might be right. "We're doing okay, just the two of us."

"You mean the three of you. Summer figures into the dynamics, and she's going to be busy over the next little while, getting settled in with Jonah. You need to get out there and start dating. You don't need to be wasting away all by your lonesome. You need a little companionship."

Guilt slammed into him. Was he expecting too much of his sister again? She was about to start her new life and he was saddling her with Polly nearly four days out of the week.

"I don't know if you noticed how lovely Cassie is looking tonight. She just got back to town and would be an interesting date, don't you think?"

And that was just what he didn't need. "Now, Ms. Lila, I don't want you to start getting your hopes up. I'm not dating. And I may not ever be ready to start dating again. Me and Polly are doing just fine."

Lila looked as if she hadn't heard a word he'd said, just stared at him with those compelling blue eyes. He stood up straighter and tried hard not to be intimidated by the little woman.

"Did I say dating? I meant friendship. Everyone could use a new friend. I know Cassie could. Someone to talk to. Now that Summer is moving in with Jonah, it's just going to be you and Polly much of the time. Speaking of which, who is taking care of Polly while you are working your shift at the fire station and Summer is gone on her honeymoon, cruising around the Bahamas?"

"We've got that handled. She is going to stay with Erin a few days and then Ms. Maryetta is going to watch her, too."

"That does sound like you have it planned out. Maybe Cassie could drop by—"

"No, ma'am. I'm asking you to please not do this. I know that you get some ideas sometimes. But honestly, I'm okay and I don't need what you're hoping for right now."

Lila sighed. "I guess I understand. So, I'll just leave you to your pink punch. It happens to be a long-time family recipe that I love to make. I'm glad to see you guarding the punch bowl so well and enjoying it like you are. Goodness knows since you aren't out there on the dance floor that you need something to pep you up, and if anything is going to do it, that's the punch to do it. It's got enough sugar in it to pep you up for a week or two."

He laughed. "I have to say, it's pink but I do love it. Polly likes it, too. She's had enough that she's bouncing off the walls. I'm probably going to be calling you all kinds of terrible names later when I'm trying to get her to settle down and go to sleep."

Lila laughed heartily at that. When she finally stopped chuckling, she winked at him. "Well, you know, it will just be a little extra daddy-daughter time. Read her a book or something to help calm her down."

"Yeah, hope so." He loved spending time with Polly but three glasses of pink punch—that he knew of—she'd probably had more before he'd realized why she was staying so close to the punch table. By the time he'd taken up his position next to it, she'd guzzled what she could. Who could blame her? The stuff was excellent.

"Talk later. Loosen up and have a good time."

He watched the blonde bombshell sashay away toward her next "victim" and hoped they were more receptive than him. If so, then maybe Lila and her buddies wouldn't start meddling in his life. Hunter shifted his attention from Lila back to the wedding party and Polly enjoying herself. On the other side of the pier from where he stood Cassie caught his eye. She had pulled out a fiberglass ladder and opened it up as if she were about to use it. Where had that come from and what was she doing? The thing had to be ten feet tall. Sure enough, she picked up her camera with the huge lens and she started up the ladder. Instantly alert to the danger of the thing toppling over, he forgot about keeping his distance and headed that way. The woman was seriously tempting fate right now. And it was something he couldn't ignore.

Hunter reached the ladder just as a kid ran straight into it, and it rocked wickedly.

Cassie gasped, looked down, and met his gaze just as the ladder toppled and she let go. One minute, she was on the ladder and the next, she was in his arms.

"Oh, wow," she gasped again.

"Gotcha." He caught her and held her securely in his arms. "I'm not sure what you were doing up there but it wasn't the best place to be." He sounded like a parent admonishing his kid, and not exactly what he wanted to sound like where she was concerned. But it hadn't been a smart move.

"I'm quite capable of figuring out what is and isn't safe for me to do. Now, if you don't mind, you can put me down now."

Why was he still holding her?

Her beautiful sea glass eyes held his. There was fire in the depths as she challenged him. "I don't mind at all, but you would have been lying on the ground if I hadn't rushed across the pier to catch you. I saw what you were doing and knew it was a setup for disaster."

"Well, aren't you the clairvoyant. I would have landed on my feet. Now set me down."

Her demand jolted him. Why was he still holding her?

She felt good in his arms and her eyes mesmerized him. His chest tightened as she squirmed to free herself. He realized that if he didn't make a move soon, she would bypass him and he would be stuck looking as though he were harassing her instead of helping her. But his arms weren't getting the message. Her brows met and her eyes darkened—with frustration, he assumed. Maybe anger.

It was in that instant reality slammed into him, and his gaze shot up and sought out Lila. Sure enough, she was watching them, a smile as wide as Texas on her face. And she wasn't alone. Her buddies, Birdie, Doreen, and Mami, stood with her, all looking as if he'd just given them exactly what they'd asked Santa Claus for Christmas.

He set Cassie on her feet.

"Thank you." She spun and stared at the fallen

ladder, then turned back. "Look, I want these shots. Look at them out there with Polly dancing and celebrating. You're going to want those shots too. Can you hold the ladder?"

Only a few moments had gone by. The song was still playing but nearing the end, and they hadn't seen the mishap between him and Cassie. He did want whatever this professional could get, and he knew Jonah and Summer would want it. "I'll do that." He reached for the ladder, stood it back up, and held it tight as she scrambled up the ladder and immediately started snapping shots.

He was stuck standing next to her very shapely bottom and legs, and trying to be unaffected by her.

And all the while wondering what Lila and her crew were grinning so big about.

* * *

Cassie tried hard not to think about the very fit man whose hard arms had caught her and held her so securely, who saved her from another fall. Thankfully, this fall was not on the same level of life-or-death as her last mishap. But it did have her questioning what in the universe was against her at the moment. After taking the photos, she might need to keep her feet planted firmly on the ground for a while.

She was more than aware of him and as she zoomed out from her brother and his bride, she caught a shot of several ladies, standing across the pier from her and looking quite smug as they watched her and Hunter. Birdie, Lila, Doreen, and Mami—those four were always into something.

The music ended and to her surprise, she saw Jonah and Summer coming their way. Polly raced to her daddy, ahead of them.

"Daddy, did you see me? I was dancing."

He laughed, a deep, pleasant sound that hummed through her like a love song to her soul—wait, what was she thinking?

"You looked like you were having a great time. I had no idea you could dance like that."

Polly beamed. "Me either. I copied Aunt Summer. And Uncle Jonah told me to just move to the music—

anything had to be better than what he was doing." She giggled. "He was right."

Jonah laughed. "Hey, don't get mean."

"I'm not. But you did look funny. Daddy—"

"Don't worry, honey, I'm not much on dancing."

Summer smiled and looked from him to Cassie. "Actually, that's why we're here. They are about to announce the brother/sister and partners dance, and since you are my only and single brother and since Cassie is Jonah's only single sibling, we wanted to request that you two dance this one together with the rest of us."

Cassie felt the earth shift—well, maybe it didn't actually shift in real life, but if it had, she wished it would open up and swallow her at that moment. They were making them dance together! She hadn't thought about dancing with the good-looking man but now that the idea had been introduced, she was right there in the moment, feeling his arms around her, and she was in so much trouble she wasn't sure what to do about it. She'd met his gaze and she felt instantly warmer—maybe she was coming down with a cold or something. Next thing she'd be feeling would be all fuzzy-headed.

Which did happen as his conflicted gaze settled on her. She could tell he was as unenthused by the idea as she was. But what could they do? This was the bride and groom.

"We can do that, can't we, Cassie?" He put the ball in her court.

"Of course we can. When?"

"Can I dance with y'all? Aunt Cassie, can I?"

"That would be great."

"Actually," Summer's eyes settled on Polly, "Grandma Maryetta wanted you to help her over at the chocolate fountain that they are getting started."

"Chocolate fountain!" Polly nearly screamed in delight. "You got one."

Summer and Jonah both laughed as she hugged them.

"You asked for it." Jonah looked delighted at Polly's beaming face.

Cassie's heart melted. Her brother was going to make an amazing father and she wondered whether they would start a family soon.

As if on cue, her mother appeared. "Polly, are you ready? We'll get this set up while all the wedding party have their dance."

"I can't wait." Polly grabbed Maryetta's hand. "You're the perfect person to show me how, because you make the best ice cream sundae I've ever had, so you will be good at putting chocolate on marshmallows."

Cassie's mom looked ecstatic at having the little girl's compliment. The music started and the DJ called out the dance. "Sounds like it's time. Now go have fun. Polly is safe with me." She placed a hand on Hunter's arm.

Cassie saw the appreciation in his eyes. "Thank you. If you need me, you'll know where to find me." He looked at Cassie as her mom and Polly walked away. "May I have this dance?"

A thrill of anticipation rippled through her. "Yes, certainly."

Yes, certainly? What kind of answer was that?

She could tell, despite his unaffected expression,

that he was bothered by the fact that they were about to dance together. She wasn't sure at all why she was so bothered, so why did it bother her that he was?

They followed Jonah and Summer out onto the designated dance area. Brad swung Lulu into his arms and she laughed as he dipped her. Nash took Erin in his arms and spoke into her ear, making her smile and kiss him. Jonah took Summer into his arms and dipped her like Brad had done with Lulu. Tate and Gigi joined them all as he twirled Gigi out and then back into his arms. Everyone was there except for Adam and Rosie, who sat on a bench together, smiling as they watched them. Rosie had her feet propped on a chair and looked beautiful with her fuller face. Pregnancy was hard on her body but looked good on her. She just couldn't get up and move around a lot.

Hunter looked at Cassie and held his hand out. "Shall we?"

She placed her hand in his and expected him to just start dancing. But he took her hand and pulled her into him, then spun her out and around before smoothly pulling her back into his arms.

She gasped as she came against him, her hand on his shoulder as his free arm twined around her waist and he held her other hand securely in his left hand. "I thought you didn't dance much?"

"I don't. I didn't say I couldn't."

Her pulse went from zero to a hundred instantly the moment his arm tightened around her and her gaze flew to his. Oh sweet peas and carrots, but the man did things to her senses that she had never felt before. He didn't move at first, just held her gaze, and she could feel his breathing quicken as she pressed against him. And then he took the first step of the slow two-step. She couldn't breathe as they moved together about the dance area. She was lost in the moment, only focused on him, and the madness that this moment was between them. She stumbled, stepped on his boot, and thankfully broke the spell his gaze had cast over her.

"Sorry." He held her steady. "I'm not as smooth as you first thought."

"Thanks for that but we both know it was me who isn't smooth."

"Okay, then let's blame it on the pier." His eyes

were shadowed.

"Fine, that sounds like a good plan." The man smelled like fresh air in a forest. She breathed him in and leaned in a little closer.

Awkward silence ensued as Jason Aldean kept singing. She tried to think of what to say. "I'm really glad you took the job at the fire department. It brought Summer here and she met Jonah."

"Yeah, it worked out well."

He kept his head up and looking straight ahead. She studied his hard jawline—better to study it than think about the feel of being in his arms. It was getting difficult to ignore the fact that he seemed as if he didn't care whether they filled in the silence or not. She told herself it was for the best that he was so obviously uninterested. But the fact that it felt so maddingly wonderful in his arms was not helping convince herself to be glad about his indifference.

* * *

Hunter felt stiff and awkward. It had been a long time

since he'd held a woman, much less on the dance floor. The last time he'd danced had been with Sandra, the night before the boating accident. And that hadn't gone well. She hadn't wanted to dance, hadn't wanted to be around him that night, and they'd argued and she'd told him she was in love with someone else and wanted a divorce. To say dancing was awkward was an understatement. To find that he liked having Cassie Sinclair in his arms was exactly what he'd been afraid of when his sister had ambushed him with this dance.

"You two make a good-looking couple." Brad grinned as he and Lulu danced by.

Lulu smiled at them. "He's right. Now, snuggle up." She winked as they two-stepped away.

Frustration dug at him. Summer knew exactly how he felt about dating or future relationships. He wasn't interested. And yet she'd done this. And now, there would be more teasing. He kept his gaze trained straight ahead, not daring to look at Cassie. He felt all eyes digging into them; he knew he'd hear about this tomorrow.

"I'm sorry this is so awkward. I can tell it wasn't

your idea of a fun time. We could end it now. I'm fine with that."

Cassie's soft, stilted words jolted him out of his thoughts. He looked down at her and in her eyes saw…what? Anger? Hurt? "It's not you." Heated shame slammed into him. "I don't mean to make you feel bad, but it is awkward for me. It's been a long time." He let out an exasperated breath. "And I wasn't expecting this." Looking at her as she stared into his eyes, his throat went dry and he fought to ignore how pretty her eyes were. His steps faltered. He wished for the song to end.

Needed it to end.

"And that makes being a block of stone okay?"

He stopped dancing just as the music ended. She stepped away from him and strode away, leaving him standing like a jerk in the center of the designated dance floor.

"What happened?" Jonah asked as he and Summer came his way, concern on their faces.

"I'm not sure. I'll go find out. I haven't danced since before Sandra's death. She probably thinks my weirdness was targeted at her. Y'all just keep celebrating and I'll go explain."

Summer touched his arm. "I'm sorry, I wasn't thinking. I shouldn't have sprung this on you."

"No, it's fine. The fact that I don't intend to date in the future doesn't mean I can't act like a normal human being. Go, have fun." He kissed her temple. "I'll be back."

Jonah put his arm around Summer. "She looks like she's heading toward the beach."

"I'm on my way."

He walked away with long strides and hoped like everything he didn't find her somewhere on the beach, crying. She didn't strike him as a person who cried much. She was, from everything he knew about her, a tough, driven career woman with big dreams and the talent that had made those dreams come true. Surely, he hadn't made her cry.

What a mess. What a jerk...

It was true, when Sandra told him she was in love with another man, they'd had angry words, and then she'd taken their child out on the boat, crashed and she'd ended up dead. Thank God Polly had been okay, had lived and was his joy, his life. But Sandra had ripped his heart out, and then, before they could even hash out what was wrong between them, she was gone. And she'd taken with her his ability to trust anyone with his heart ever again. He had no desire to ever put himself through that again. There was so much baggage there, so many wounds that cut deep and hadn't even been dragged out into the light. He just knew he'd loved his wife, been betrayed, and now he was obviously a present-day jerk.

He raked a hand through his hair and scanned the beach as he reached the area just past the low dunes. He spotted her sitting on the sand, just beyond the reach of the water. She had her legs drawn up and her arms hugged them. She'd kicked off her shoes and they lay flipped upside down on the white sugar sand. Her hair ruffled in the breeze. Her pretty profile looked starkly sad.

He felt sick at heart. Had he become that stone-cold that he insulted a woman just because he was attracted to her and didn't want to be?

CHAPTER THREE

Cassie would not cry. What was wrong with her, anyway? She'd been like this ever since the accident and she wasn't sure what to do about it.

She'd had narrow escapes before and shaken it off and gone on about her business. This time, it had shaken her and hung on.

The icy cold shoulder Hunter had given her, after the promising first few steps of the dance, had just been more than her already strained emotional state of mind could take. So what if the firefighter wasn't the most pleasant guy around? She wasn't going to stick around anyway…was she?

"Cassie, mind if I sit down?"

His husky, masculine voice sent a defense-lowering shiver racing through her. She turned her head to find him bent slightly at the waist to get closer to her to speak. She literally lost her breath at his unexpected nearness.

"It's still a free country and I don't own the beach." She faced the big blue ocean again and did not feel any better despite her sassy comeback to him.

He settled beside her, not worrying about his dress slacks and the sand. She'd been the same about her dressy navy jumper but was too upset to care. He planted the heels of his dress shoes in the sand and propped his elbows on his raised knees. She was very aware of every inch of the man beside her.

"I apologize for my behavior back there."

His solemn, sincere words washed over her and she fought not to let them make a dent in her aggravation.

"I know it's not an excuse but that was the first time I've danced since the last time I danced with my late wife. It was unexpected and I behaved badly."

His words broke through her defenses like a bull moose in a china store, shattering everything.

That dug deep into her I-don't-care-about-him attempted attitude.

"I'm sorry about your wife. I'm sure that was hard, this being sprung on us like it was."

"Yeah, not that they meant anything by it. Summer wouldn't do that, wouldn't want it to be a problem for me. Jonah either. They were just trying to get all of the family out there on the dance floor. I should have behaved better. Do you forgive me?"

She couldn't remember the last time a man had asked forgiveness of her. She had brothers, and they were great, but asking for her forgiveness was not something that had ever crossed their minds growing up. Not that they had done anything to warrant asking her such a thing. In her line of work, men didn't think in those terms either…again, not that she expected any such thing. "There's nothing to forgive. Seriously, it's fine. I'm fine."

He looked thoughtful, then picked up a shell out in

front of him and rolled it between his strong, blunt-nailed fingers. She watched him finger the shell and butterflies fluttered in her chest. He had strong hands, used for saving lives. She remembered how his touch felt moments before and warmth filled her. What was wrong with her?

He threw the shell out into the soft waves. As the evening moved on, they were getting stronger but for now were soothing to her soul.

He suddenly tilted his head and studied her. "What's going on then? If you didn't need my apology, if my behavior isn't what put that troubled expression in your eyes and on your face, then something did. Something is bothering you. If it's not me, then what? Or aren't you being truthful with me, and I did put that strain in your eyes?"

How did he do that? She propped an elbow on her knee and rubbed her temple with her fingertips, trying to ease the tension pounding there. She sighed. "I just have some work-related issues."

"Do you need to talk about it?"

"No. No, I'm fine."

He hitched a brow, looking as if he didn't believe her.

She might need to talk about it but she didn't need to talk to him about it. Couldn't talk to him—could she? Shifting her gaze away, she stared out at the blue water. The music from the wedding shifted to something livelier and she glanced that way, to her family having such a good time. She couldn't worry them. Wouldn't worry them, at least not right now. "You can't tell anyone. My parents and my brothers would have a fit. I had an accident before I came here. A clip came loose and I fell."

His expression hardened. "You fell? Wait—you do weird shoots, like you hang off the side of things with that camera of yours. You fell off of what?"

This was a mistake. She shouldn't have said anything. "It's nothing."

"No, really...tell me. I promise I won't tell anyone. You fell off of what? Were you hurt?"

"My pride and my mentality. I fell, not far. About five feet. My other harness held. I had security measures in place. I don't do the shoots as a death wish or anything, so we take precautions. But it messed with my head. I'm still a little shook up. I had planned to come home for the wedding, so I took some extra time off."

"Yeah, I would think something like that would mess with your head a bit. How did it happen? Did you put the clip in? Do you know how to do that?"

"Yes, I know how to do that. And no, my crew put the clip in. It was an accident. Clips come out sometimes. That's where precautions kick in."

"Someone was careless. Someone should have made sure that it was safe. They don't come loose that often."

Okay, maybe she shouldn't have said anything to him. "Relax. I told you because I thought you might understand. I thought you wanted to be a sounding board or something, but just forget it." She started to stand but he grabbed her arm and held her in place. She glared at him and he glared right back.

"No, wait. Hold on. Yeah, I'm reacting because I care. Your brothers would care. You can't tell me that you almost lost your life and not expect me to react.

You need to tell your family this."

"Don't tell me that. I shouldn't have told you. Just forget it. I'm fine. I had precautions. This is my job—I'm not some child. In your job, you take all the precautions you can, but still, sometimes things go wrong. It's not that that's bothering me, it's…I've had close calls before."

His eyes darkened and she realized again that she should stop rambling and keep her mouth shut.

"You've had accidents before? Now I'm really worried. Did your crew set that up for you too?"

"Look, I have a competent crew."

They stared at each other as the seconds ticked by. On the one hand, it was nice that he cared but on the other, it was him, a total stranger. Why she'd even told him this much was a mystery. She never told anyone about things that went wrong with her job. For one, her brothers were overprotective and would probably try to lock her in a trunk somewhere to keep her safe. It didn't matter if they did things that were sometimes sketchy. Tate would have a cow, even though he'd recently had an accident doing a movie stunt. Still, it wouldn't be the same if he found out about her accident. And he'd probably rip her crew's heads off, just like Hunter looked as if that's what he wanted to do.

"So, at least you're okay but things can mess with your head. I've been there, kind of still there myself. I'm working my way out of it but things don't always turn around like you want them to."

What was she thinking? The man had lost his wife. Lost her to a terrible tragedy and almost lost his daughter in the same boating accident. And here she was, getting mad at him because he was questioning her safety protocols. Remorse and guilt filled her.

"I'm so sorry. No wonder you're reacting this way. After having lost your wife to a tragedy, I can see why you would react so hard. Erin told me about what happened with your wife. I'm so sorry, for you and Polly. To lose someone you love so suddenly, so tragically—you know full well what loss is. Are you doing better?"

He stared out at the water, not saying anything for a long time. "For the most part, I'm okay but things hit me. And then…there are things that most people don't know. Brad knows the whole story but…never mind. It does no good to rehash the past."

Now he had her curiosity up. "What things?" She blurted out the question despite knowing how rude it was. But she did it anyway. He was a stranger; they just met, and yet she wanted to know. What was wrong with her?

"It's a long, screwed-up story and some things aren't as it seems. Believe me, I learned that the hard way. I guess life just throws you curve balls sometimes. Anyway, we better get back, if you feel better. If you don't want to talk more. I know you aren't going to tell your family, though I think you should. But I told them I'd come find you and check on you and bring you back to the dance. I won't be dancing anymore, even if Summer requests it. Are you okay?"

He must have loved his wife very much. How long had it been? Three years, she thought Erin had said. That wasn't that long to mourn. Some of the things he'd said had her curious about what had happened but she wasn't one to snoop. At least not too much. And yet she couldn't help being curious. She couldn't imagine if she were loved like that by someone and then lost them, that she could move forward. If she had died on that mountain, no one would have mourned her like he mourned his wife. This made her deeply sad for him and that was part of her mindset right now…she hadn't known that kind of love. "I'm fine. I guess it just hit me. The whole wedding thing. I shouldn't have been out there dancing either. I'm going to get over this and then I'm going to get back to work. I'll be fine. Thanks for listening. And thanks for keeping it a secret. Please."

"You shared it with me in confidence. It's not my story to tell but I'm sure your family would want to know. They care about you. They'd want to be there for you."

"I know they would, but then the next time I went out to do my thing, they'd really be worried. They have adjusted to the somewhat risky things I do but they don't know about it until the pictures come out. You know, sometimes after the fact is easier. If they have an illusion that there wasn't really a danger, then it's easier on them."

He didn't look convinced, but he gave a nod of acquiescence. "Again, it's your story to tell. Okay, let's get you back."

He stood and held his hand out to her. She stared at the very strong, capable hand and then lifted hers and slipped it into his. Immediately, his fingers wrapped around hers and sent a shiver of warm awareness coursing through her. This man was dangerous to her.

He tugged and she rose to stand very close to him. That masculine scent wrapped around her. They stared at each other and both took a step away from each other in the next instant.

"Thanks." She pulled her hand from his.

"You're welcome." They started back toward the pier and the wedding merriment. He paused, and took a step back to pick up her sandals. They dangled from his fingers as he held them out to her.

She reached for them; their fingers brushed and awareness warmed through her like a fire flame being fanned. She pulled the shoes away and smiled, trying hard to act as if she wasn't affected. She probably failed miserably. Nothing had happened. She was just not thinking straight and obviously, this was not the guy to even consider thinking about testing out the thoughts strumming through her mind. She was not meant for picket fences and settling down. Even if her brain was sending out those crazy thoughts, if she gave it a week or two, she'd be back to normal. She'd go back to her life; she'd be happy again.

She just needed time.

* * *

They reached the pier just in time for Cassie to get swept up into the throwing of the bouquet. When she saw Summer standing in front of the group of single ladies, she waved at Cassie to come join them.

Cassie stopped short.

He could almost feel her panic. "Not a fan of the flower toss?"

"I'm fine with it. I just don't want to be involved

in it." Her voice had risen slightly and she took a step backward.

"Cassie, I'm glad I spotted you." Mami Desmond was breathless as she hurried toward them. The older woman was a powerhouse and she usually did not take no for an answer. "We've been waiting on you. Honey, put those sandals on and get out there. You might get lucky." She smiled at Hunter, and there was no way around the fact that he was included in the "get lucky" statement.

Hunter resisted the urge to run a finger around the collar of his shirt, remembering seeing Mami and her group of ladies watching him and Cassie earlier. Were they thinking what he feared they were thinking—that the poor widower and the famous photographer were a match? The almost panicked look Cassie shot him told him explicitly that she was not interested in that plan.

"Mami, I'm not, I don't..." Cassie stuttered.

Mami just laughed. "Come on, girl. You're not about to get eaten by the boogie monster. It's just a bouquet. Come on."

Hunter watched in dismay as Mami took Cassie's

arm and obviously would have pretty much dragged Cassie to the group of single ladies. But Cassie, after putting her sandals back on, went with her without making a scene. He felt really bad for her, but more than that, he wondered how messed up she was. He told himself that it wasn't his business, that she would fill him in on the main reason she was struggling if she wanted to. Not that he wanted to be involved, but he couldn't deny that he was curious.

He heard his name called and glanced over his shoulder to where his daughter was waving beside the cake. He shot another look at Cassie, who looked resigned to her fate now. Even with a smile on her face, not a big one but still a smile. He admired her because he knew she truly didn't want to be in the group and yet to make a scene would take the joy out of the event of his sister and her brother's happy day. She was cool that way, in his book.

Turning away, he strode through the crowd to where Polly stood beside Maryetta, overseeing the wedding cake.

"Look, Daddy. I cut the cake. Do you want a

piece?" Polly's smile and excitement lit up his world.

"You did a great job. Of course I want cake. Have you ever seen me not take a piece of cake?"

His daughter giggled in that sweet, heart-tingling way that she giggled and it warmed his heart. Then the chill of how close he'd come to losing her yanked at him. The dark days after losing her mom and the anger he'd felt that her mother had very nearly taken her from him. No one, not even Brad, knew the extent of what had happened in that accident. He tried to concentrate on the joy her giggles brought him instead of the fear of almost losing her that haunted him. He took the cake. "It looks wonderful."

She gazed adoringly up at him. Oh, the love of a child. "It's yummy, Daddy. Grandma Maryetta let me have some and I loved it. She is the best."

Maryetta looked delighted at the praise and smiled a beautiful smile. The older woman had a vivacious attitude and was just a lovely lady in all aspects. Warm, generous, and also driving her family a bit bonkers in her quest of wanting grandchildren. She'd been delighted for Polly to join the family through

Jonah and Summer. They had all been so good to Polly since the first day they arrived. He was so grateful to Maryetta and Leo, all the Sinclairs.

"Of course, I let Polly have a bite. I even had a bite. And we've decided that this cake is so big that there will surely be leftovers, so be forewarned that you'll have some heading home with you."

Polly looked gleeful. "We're taking it home with us."

He chuckled. "I won't complain." He took the plate she held out to him, took the fork, and got a forkful of the white cake and a hunk of creamy white icing. He took the bite and it melted in his mouth.

"Good, isn't it?" Polly asked.

"Oh yeah. You are so right."

"Look, Polly…Aunt Summer is throwing the bouquet. You have time to run over there and jump in." Maryetta winked at her.

"Oh, no." Polly giggled again. "Daddy won't let me get married yet. Besides, Aunt Summer married Uncle Jonah, so I can't take him from her."

"So now I know…it's Uncle Jonah?"

"Well, Daddy, he's older than me but he's so nice and…he did help me get back in a boat and go out on the water again. You know, Daddy, we need to try that again. We haven't been back on a boat since then and you said we would. I think I'm ready to do that again."

He stilled his heart, trying to quiet the thundering that started anytime she mentioned getting back on the water. Jonah had helped Polly get back on the water, and he would be forever grateful to him for that. Hunter hadn't attempted to take her back in a boat after the accident that had almost taken her away from him. But they had planned to continue to try and get her completely over the nightmares that plagued her that had to do with her in the water so long after the boat crash. But he hadn't been able to follow through. The trauma of the day still got to her and that got to him. He had his own issues because of everything. She was seeing a therapist and that had helped, but there were times when she still woke in the night screaming his name, worried that he, too, had drowned in that horrible accident, leaving her to float alone in the water that she had once loved so dearly until rescue teams made it to her.

"That sounds like a plan. I did promise you that."

She smiled. "Good. Then maybe we can do that soon. I think I'm ready."

He nodded. But the question of whether he was ready remained. Could he endure the panic he felt? His job was rescuing people but every time he thought about his baby out there alone in that water with only a life vest between her survival and her death, he got physically ill. It was his Achilles heel and it had at times paralyzed him. It was something he was going to have to overcome. Living in fear was not the way anyone needed to live and the only way to get over it was to face it head on. And that was what his brave little child was trying to do.

How could he not do the same?

He watched as Summer held the bouquet high then flung it over her head. It hurtled through the air and landed straight into the unexpecting arms of Cassie. Poor Cassie, facing her own fears, or trying. Or running. He wasn't sure what she was doing. She'd only raised her hands in self-defense because it would have hit her in the face if she hadn't caught it. Now, looking stunned, she held the flowers in her hands as everyone around her cheered, so happy for her. But it was obvious—to him, at least—that anything to do with the bouquet was very problematic for her.

He wondered again what that was all about.

He realized very clearly that he and she could have something very much in common.

CHAPTER FOUR

The morning after the wedding, Cassie walked from her room at her mom and dad's house and found her mom sitting at the kitchen counter with a travel brochure spread out on the bar. She filled a mug with coffee then padded over to sit across from her mom.

"The wedding was really lovely last night."

"I thought so. They are a wonderful couple and I'm thrilled for them." Maryetta took a sip of her coffee. "And I'm excited that you caught the bouquet."

"It was that or have it hit me in the face. A reflex,

really, was all it was." That was the truth. She should have just sidestepped and let the flowers hurtle past and into Shanna Prue's waiting arms. Shanna had been trying to snag a man since they'd all graduated and was having no luck. From what the rumor mill said, she was just trying too hard. Not that catching a bouquet really helped because she heard some of the ladies whispering last night after the toss that Shanna pretty much held the record for catching the bouquet and it hadn't worked yet.

Which Cassie found comforting, because she had no business catching the thing in the state of mind she was in. Her heart was doing that strange lean toward wanting a true love before her time on earth expired, but her mind was telling her that she wanted what she'd always wanted: adventure, fame for the best photos out there, and the freedom to go where she wanted, when she wanted, no strings attached. She was not trusting her heart in this.

She glanced over to the side table near the entrance of the back door, where she'd placed the bouquet when she'd come inside last night. It could stay there. She should have given it to Shanna to add to her collection. From what the ladies said in that same conversation, the poor woman hung the bouquets upside down and let the flowers dry and now had no telling how many dried wedding bouquets.

"Do you think Shanna Prue really does have a collection of wedding bouquets?"

Her mom nodded. "Oh, yes. Lila and Doreen saw them."

"That's just odd. I should give her Summer's."

"No, you keep it. Just hang it upside down and let it dry out."

"I don't think so. I'm not going into competition with Shanna on the dried bouquets. What in the world is she going to do with them?"

"Mami said she's trying for some kind of Guinness Book of World Record. I think she's aiming at that more than finding a husband these days."

"I guess we all have to have our own path." Cassie picked up a brochure from the counter. "Are you thinking of taking a cruise to Alaska?"

Her mom beamed at her and leaned forward with a

joyful expression. "Yes, actually. We have had a great offer. We hope to leave the day after tomorrow." Her mother's excitement was clear as her eyes sparkled.

"Wow, that soon." That meant her parents weren't going to be here while she was in town. She wasn't sure whether her spirits should hurt by that, but then, it would give her some time alone to really figure things out and maybe she needed that. "I'm excited for you."

Her mom reached across and cupped Cassie's hands between hers. "This has come as such a surprise. I know you just got here, but you'll have Erin, Lulu, and Rosie, and Gigi. And Summer when they get back. It's just so thrilling to have all these wonderful new additions to the family. And you'll have your brothers, too. Just take over the house and maybe throw a girls' night out for all of you. That would be fun. You're never home and this is just a fantastic time for you to bond with everyone. And Polly, such a sweetie! Oh, how I adore and love her. Speaking of which...I wanted to talk to you. I was supposed to watch Polly a few days while Summer and Jonah are on their honeymoon. Erin is going to be able to help some, too, but would you mind giving her a hand if she needs you? Everyone else has something going on, and I thought maybe you would have fun. She is no trouble and adorable. And Hunter isn't working every day. Just three days on, then three days off, and then it repeats."

She blinked, shocked by the whole sudden change of events that had happened in the last five minutes. She'd gone from just hanging out and having a good visit with her parents and her family, to her parents abandoning her and her babysitting Hunter Claremont's little girl. And her mother was asking her to fill in for her…it wasn't something she could say no to. Her parents had always wanted to go on an Alaskan cruise and who was she to stand in their way? Besides that, she had the time. After all, she would be twiddling her thumbs before the day was over—downtime was not something she did. She liked to stay busy.

But Hunter Claremont… She would be in contact with the man who unsettled her in the most confusing ways.

The back door opened, and footsteps sounded on the tile. "Hello, it's Erin," her sister called just before appearing from the hallway. She smiled when she saw them at the kitchen counter. "Perfect. Just the two I'm looking for."

"Oh yeah?" Her mom pat the stool beside her. "Come sit down and tell us. You look really excited."

Erin placed both hands flat on the granite counter, her eyes dancing. "Nash has just been invited on a two-week book tour in Europe for his latest book. It's going crazy over there like it did here, and you know I didn't get to go with him on that tour, so—this is just really exciting—I'm going with him." Her gaze shifted to Cassie. "If, that is, you can pinch-hit for me and watch Polly?"

Cassie had been excited for her sister; first her mom and now Erin. What was going on?

"Meaning you want me to keep Polly by myself for two weeks, not just help out?"

Erin nodded slowly, hope in her eyes. "I wouldn't normally dream of imposing on you like this but it happened so fast and it is such a great opportunity.

And I really want to go. I love Polly to death but this is an opportunity I just hate to miss. I can have someone come in and watch over my bed-and-breakfast but I can't trust just anyone with Polly. I agreed to help out—and I will—if you can't do this, I would completely understand. You had your time home planned out, so just tell me and I'll stay."

Her mom and Erin both stared at her with their breaths held. She knew she didn't want to do this but how could she refuse. They both stared at her as though she were their only hope. Again, how in the world had this happened? Conspiracy theories flew into her thoughts. But no, that couldn't be so. They wouldn't set something like this up to connive her into watching Hunter's child. No, it was simply not in them to do that. It was just a coincidence that all this hit at the same time. Meant to be? No, not meant to be either. It was just what it was: a coincidence, and a good thing for them that she was free and able to take up the slack for them.

She nodded, slowly, as if preparing herself before she spoke. "Yes, I'll do it. It's just a little girl. How hard can it be?"

Her mom and her sister both grabbed her hands at the same time and they all stared at one another with their hands piled together. She fought to make sure her eyes seemed as happy as could be; she didn't want them to know how hard a time she was having to force enthusiasm for this. It wasn't Polly; it was the thought of spending so much time with Hunter. She had told him things she hadn't told anyone and still didn't know why she'd opened up to him a little.

This was going to be hard.

"Are you sure I can do this? I've never been around kids."

Her mother patted her arm. "Of course you can. Polly is wonderful. She's an old soul in a little bitty body. She'll be teaching you things before you know it. And she loves to bake. You love to bake, though you don't get to do it on the road. This will be your chance. Enjoy...have fun. The poor dear, after losing her mom so tragically, she gets sad sometimes, so you have to boost her up, but for the most part she's very brave and happy. Summer has told me that she has nightmares sometimes and it really disturbs her daddy. He's worried about her. That's one reason they are here in a small town, so he can be close to her most of the time. We've just fallen in love with both of them. You're going to have a good time and he's so handsome. Who knows...I saw you on the beach with him last night from where I was by the cake, and you two looked like you were having a good conversation."

"Mom, we had a conversation and we danced because Summer wanted us to. I'm not on the market, and he isn't either. I'm pretty sure he's still in love with his wife. I could see that he was crazy about her and disturbed when we talked about her—"

"You talked about his wife?" Erin looked shocked.

"Not a lot but she did come up, just a touch. He seems emotionally distant. And besides, I don't need him to be emotionally distant or available. I'll watch Polly and that's that."

"You do that." Erin winked at her. "And maybe you can help him become emotionally present. Who knows...maybe this is meant to be? You can have a little fun while you're home. It's a little adventure of sorts, here at home."

"I agree, wholeheartedly," her mother cooed, looking far more delighted than was comfortable for Cassie.

She warily watched her mom tapping her long fingers on the granite as she thought. "I would just love it if you fell in love with someone from Sunset Bay and settled down here with the rest of your family."

Oh, dear goodness, what was happening? "You two need to calm down. I'm committing to standing in for the two of you, but you're putting a lot of pressure on me now for things that I am not enthused about at all. I will watch this sweet little girl. But I repeat, do not get any ideas about me and Hunter Claremont. I don't care how good-looking the guy is. Or how emotionally traumatized he is. Maybe he needs someone to help him get over all of that but—I repeat—that is not me."

Her sister's and her mom's gazes met conspiratorially and she could tell that she had not made a dent in what they were thinking. She had been through this before. These two had ganged up on her once before when they'd decided that she and poor Dex Carpenter, who as far as she knew was still a fireman at the station with Hunter and Brad, were a match. They had pushed and pushed and she had not fallen for the guy. He was great, handsome, nice, and yet she had plans of her own and falling in love had not been part of it. She was still embarrassed when she ran into him on trips back home. She had to basically break his heart and that had not felt good. Thankfully, he hadn't been at the wedding last night so she'd at least avoided that meet-up for a little while. He had confessed his love for her several times and despite how wonderful he was, it had been embarrassing to tell him she wasn't interested in settling down. She'd hoped at some point he would find someone to knock him off his feet with an amazing love story. But as far as she knew, he was still single, just like she planned to remain.

She shook herself. "You two stop looking at me like that. You are not going to do with me what you did with Dex. So get that out of your heads."

They both had the decency to look apologetic.

"Okay, settle down. It's true we went overboard." Erin sighed. "But I adore Hunter and what he's doing to help his little girl get over her trauma. You can't blame me for hoping that something might come of you two. He's a great guy. And you wanted that for me, too. But until Nash came along and swept me off my feet, I was like you. So I was hoping the same thing for you. And Hunter is awesome."

Her mom agreed. "He truly is. I, too, had thought you and Dex would be great together. He's a great guy and who knows, maybe this is your time. Maybe all those years ago just was the wrong time. But no, I'm not going to push you two together again. But he does ask about you all the time. I think he's still in love with you. So there are two amazing guys for you to pick from."

"You two need to stop."

Erin's expression grew pained. "It's not that easy. Dex does ask about you, so it's not just us thinking these thoughts. Everyone is."

"Everyone?"

"Yes, Lila Peabody and—"

"And Mami and Doreen and Birdie?" She groaned inwardly. They'd all been watching her and Hunter last night. So they were all hoping she would fall for one or the other or— "Who is everyone rooting for?"

Erin bit her lip and grimaced. "Hunter, since it's him and Polly. They're a sweet package."

Oh, it was worse than she'd feared. "If and when I do fall in love, I don't need any help." There, she'd said it firmly.

"We just love you, honey."

"I know, but I have my own life."

Erin smiled. "Of course you do. And I get that. So, relax. I'll be roaming about Europe with my amazing husband, and I won't have time to worry about you, and Mom will be focusing on her Alaskan cruise. And you'll be here with two different handsome men and one adorable little girl. Who knows what the future will bring?"

Oh, my word. She read right through that song and dance. What was she going to do with them? She shook her head and laughed at their irritating antics. "You two better hope I don't pack up and leave town tonight."

Her mom laughed. "You wouldn't do that. You know how much these trips mean to us and you are not the type to dash our dreams, so your bluff is not working."

Shoot, she did not have a poker face. She gave up. "When do I officially start? Oh, and did you ask him? Does he know I'm taking your places? Will he trust me with his child?"

"Yes, he'll trust you," Erin said.

"Of course he knows you're trustworthy." Her mother looked shocked that she would even suggest he might not trust her.

She had a feeling they might be wrong. He hadn't exactly given off vibes that he was thrilled about being around her either.

And now they were going to be stuck with each other for at least two weeks.

Her pulse jumped just thinking about it.

* * *

"Y-you're not going to watch Polly?" Hunter repeated the words as if he wasn't functioning on all cylinders, as if he'd just woken up after a night of almost no sleep—which was exactly what he had done only an hour earlier.

Erin smiled at him apologetically. "That's right. I'm so sorry. I've had this opportunity to go with Nash on a book tour across Europe. But all is well, because Cassie is here and has agreed to step in for me. It will be perfect. Also, Mom and Dad are going on an Alaskan cruise. They've always wanted to go and a couple of friends invited them along, so they're going. See, Cassie being here is perfect. She's going to stay here with Polly. They'll be fast friends before you know it. They both are adventurous and love to bake, so inside or outside they'll get along great." She paused, but when he didn't speak, his mind reeling from the news, she continued, "She's very capable. She can handle traveling all around the world by herself half the time, so you can trust that she'll be good for watching Polly. She's one of the most capable, trustworthy people I know," she repeated, as if to make sure he got that part.

He'd gotten it. "I don't have any doubt about that. But, she said she'd do it?"

"Yes, she said she would be glad to do it. She's always been good about helping out the family when her schedule allowed it or when she had enough notice to rearrange her schedule. This time it just worked out, as if it was meant to be. I mean, everything has just fallen into place like puzzle pieces."

He wasn't so sure it was as perfect as they anticipated but what choice did he have? He wasn't going to ask Maryetta not to go on her cruise and he couldn't ask Erin not to go on a book tour to Europe with her famous husband. That both of these major opportunities happened when he needed them was a bit of a shocker, but he would get over it. And so, he guessed for the next two weeks, he was going to be stuck with Cassie. Or she would probably say that she was stuck with him, because he was fairly sure that she had had no other options but to do this or be responsible for her mom and sister missing out on their trips. He had seen her stand in the bouquet toss and smile when she had not wanted to be there. But for the good of her brother and his sister, she'd danced with him and caught the bouquet. So now she was watching his child.

Erin was right about one thing—when possible, Cassie did step in for her family.

"We leave before daylight, so I won't see you tomorrow. But Cassie will start tomorrow afternoon before you head to your shift at the firehouse."

"Okay." He was still trying to figure it all out. She would be spending the night here at the house with Polly for the three nights he was on shift. Polly had been going to stay at Erin's bed-and-breakfast before. But he did have Summer's room, so having her here was no problem as far as a bedroom. But...

"You look a bit overwhelmed." Erin's gaze grew worried. "Cassie will be staying at Mom's when she's not here, and she'll have her car so she and Polly can go to the beach or looking for sea turtles and manatees like Polly likes to do. Summer said she absolutely loves sea creatures and being near the water."

"Yes, that's right. She always has. But, Cassie doesn't have a problem staying here?"

Erin smiled, as if she were finally in on the secret. "No, you'll be gone, so there isn't anything wrong with it. People of Sunset Bay know you're a fireman and you have weird hours and need help with your little girl. They could stay at Mom and Dad's but it would probably be easier on Polly to stay in her own home. This is fine."

"Okay, then it's a go. I'm glad you're getting to do this with Nash. And your mom and dad too."

Erin smiled and gave him a hug. "Yes, and thank you for understanding."

He liked Erin and Nash a lot. They were a great couple and had, like the others of the Sinclair family, become good friends. This was a good trip for them. And he had had Cassie on his mind ever since the wedding. They hadn't gotten to talk any after the bouquet toss but he had wondered about her several times over the last twenty-four hours.

Whether he wanted to admit it or not, he was looking forward to seeing her again.

And that was the thing that worried him the most.

CHAPTER FIVE

Hunter was waiting outside his house, watching Polly swing, when Cassie drove her white BMW SUV into his driveway. All day, he had fought feeling nervous about seeing her again. It wasn't like him to get nervous. He entered burning buildings for a living, and had less nerves doing that than he felt as she pulled to a halt and then got out of her vehicle.

"Look, Daddy, Aunt Cassie is here." Polly jumped from the swing while it was still halfway in the air. She landed on her feet and raced toward Cassie as she was closing the car door. "Hi, Aunt Cassie."

"Hi, Polly. You were just amazing, jumping off of that swing."

Polly smiled proudly. "My daddy says I'm like a cat and I always land on my feet. I really am."

"Hi, Cassie. My daughter's confidence isn't lacking, as you can see."

Cassie smiled. "Hi. I think I have to agree with your dad."

"I can teach you how to do it. We're going to have fun." Polly reached for Cassie's hand and tugged her toward the swing.

"Hang on," he said. "You can show Cassie how to jump out of a swing later. We need to show her where everything is in the house first. And you might be surprised but Cassie might already know how to jump out of a swing. She climbs on the side of mountains and jumps out of airplanes and things like that."

Shock rocked Polly's face. Her eyes flared wide. "You jump out of airplanes? And climb mountains?"

"I do. When I need to for my job, but jumping off of a swing might be different, so I'll need you to show me how you do it before I try it. It's always good to get pointers from the expert before you do something new."

"I'll show you then, after Daddy leaves for the fire station. Aunt Erin told me you would be fun. So did Grandma Maryetta when we were cutting the cake at the wedding."

"She told you at the wedding I was fun?"

Polly nodded. "Yes, when she asked me if I would like you to keep me."

"Oh, I see. Well, I hope I don't disappoint."

Polly smiled sweetly. "You won't. Come on, this way to the house." Polly still held her hand and pulled her toward the front steps. "You're going to be fun. And I like your hair."

Cassie's hand lifted to touch the gentle curls that hung to her shoulders. "Thank you. It's natural. I don't have to do a lot to it, which makes me a little bit lazy when it comes to styling my hair. I like your curls too."

Polly giggled. "Me too. I think when I grow up I'll be lazy too."

They both laughed.

Hunter smiled, seeing that they were going to get

along so well. Exactly like Erin had said they would. He liked Cassie's gentle ways too. And he had found himself a time or two wanting to touch her hair and see whether it was as soft as it looked. He reminded himself immediately to keep his hands to himself. Touching her was the last thing he needed to do. Thoughts of their dance reminded him immediately how good it had felt to hold her…he shook the thought off and opened the door to the house.

"Ladies first." He smiled easily as Cassie met his gaze. There was worry there, too. Probably very similar to his. He and she both knew there was a tension that tugged between them, and he had the feeling she was at war with it as much as he was. As she passed by him, his pulse raced out of control and he followed her and Polly inside. He was happy that at least Polly was thrilled about the situation.

Polly chattered away as she led Cassie down the hall toward the living room and kitchen area. He smiled, listening to them, knowing that this was good. Polly was excited and happy and that was what it was all about these days.

"Come on, I'll show you my room." Polly took Cassie's hand and led her through the living room to the door that led to her room.

He went to the kitchen and got a glass out of the cabinet and filled it with water from the refrigerator. He took a long drink, glad this was going to work out for Polly. He wondered what Cassie would think of his home. Summer had helped decorate so that it would be bright and inviting for a young girl. Also so that Polly would remember her life before the accident, that it was happy and she was loved. There were pictures of all of them on the walls and scattered around on some of the tables.

He barely looked at the walls. He wondered again what Cassie would think.

Why he was wondering this, he didn't know. He had learned his lesson about giving your heart to someone; to have it ripped out and shredded was no fun. The devastation it could leave on someone's heart wasn't worth it to him. He knew some people said it was, but he didn't feel that way. He was hardened where love was concerned. It didn't matter that, for some reason, Cassie Sinclair had slipped right over a protective barrier he'd erected before he had even realized she was doing it. It was worrisome. Then again, it didn't matter because he had upped his guard. This was only about Polly. Everything in his life was about Polly. Including these pictures on the walls that he barely glanced at.

He'd learned that it was okay for a man to focus everything on the good of his child. It was a safe place to be. And for a guy who entered burning buildings and had a few times walked out on ledges to rescue people, his life had once felt like that. It had fallen apart in a disastrous way, burned down, and fallen off cliffs. No, he wasn't going back to that. He took a sip of water as laughter came from Polly's room. He wasn't doing that again. It was all about that right there—his daughter laughing again and having a good life. That was all he cared about.

Nothing else mattered. And he would do what he needed to do to keep her safe from any more heartache in her life, too.

* * *

Cassie followed Polly out of her room. The house was pretty. Colorful and lived in. There were leather chairs, and a buff-toned couch with small pinstripes of red throughout it and colorful pillows of reds and blues to bring out the color of the couch, and rugs on the hardwood floors. Polly's room was pink with purple and yellow and very adorable. She was fairly positive that Summer had done the decorating. Summer was an artist and this had her touch all over it. She had an eye for color but also for making it homey. She had no idea how creative Hunter was, but she had plenty of brothers and they would never have decorated like this. She was betting that Hunter had given Summer free rein to decorate this house and make it a home for him and his little girl.

But all of that was secondary to the photos. They were sprinkled everywhere. Big photos and small photos sitting on tables. Many of them were of Polly. Many were of Polly and Hunter. But most of them were of Hunter and Polly with a beautiful brunette with curly hair who looked very much like Polly. They all showed a beautiful, active, loving life that they'd all shared prior to the tragedy that had stolen her from Hunter and Polly. It made Cassie sad to see the vibrant woman and know that she was no longer with the family she so obviously loved. She tried hard not to stare at Hunter in the photos but she couldn't help it; he was more relaxed-looking, happy in them. There was a tangible difference in his expression now and she could not put her finger on it. Obviously, he was in love with his wife, his family, his life. For those years in those photos, he had it all. That was it. That was what she saw there.

As a photographer, she tried to grab snapshots of life for people. And overall, looking at these shots, that was the feeling she got when she looked into his eyes.

He was a man at the top of the world in these photos.

That was missing now. There was a wariness, almost, in his eyes when he looked at her. A sadness, maybe?

Though she was young in the photos, Polly had

been active. She was fishing and smiling. Always smiling. She was driving a boat—with her dad's help but in her element on the water. They had loved being on the water; it was clearly evident. And Sandra, she believed that was her name, had been an avid fisherman and stunning.

As she met his gaze across the room, it was a good reminder that he still loved his wife. Not that one ever did fully recover from the loss of a loved one, or stop loving them. But they did move on, eventually, and it was clear by his reactions on the beach the night of the wedding and through these photos that Hunter clearly hadn't moved on yet. Not that it should matter to her.

She was here to do a job. To do a job she wasn't completely comfortable doing. But it was for her mother and her sister. The more she thought about it, the more she was fairly certain she had been ramrodded into this by a careful plan. It hadn't all just miraculously fallen into place. They'd had a week to plan things after she'd let them know she was coming. Her mother didn't just happen to throw an Alaskan cruise together but a week of knowing she was extending her stay…it could be planned in a week. And Erin had probably wanted to go on this trip with Nash but had committed to keeping Polly, so it hadn't been possible until Cassie had decided to extend her visit. Yes, she had been had. But the truth was that they had needed her. It was unfortunate that the scare on the side of the mountain had made her extend the stay. Instead of just extending it because she wanted to or should have was not important in this instance. She was here and glad to help them so they could do these amazing trips.

She was just going to have to get her head on straight over the next two weeks and not let the butterflies that overcame her when she was near Hunter overtake her. She could not let these thoughts she'd been having about Hunter get her into trouble.

She would be here for three days, and he would be at work. When he was off work, she would go back to her parents' home and not see him. She would only see him before he went to work and after he got off. Things would be fine. This would work out.

Their gazes met across the room like a bulldozer

careening into her and reminded her immediately that it wasn't as easy as she was trying desperately to convince herself it would be.

"I gave Aunt Cassie the tour." Polly climbed up onto a barstool and grinned at her daddy. "She likes my room. She likes all my pictures, too. I showed her Mama and us fishing and on the beach in the boat. She liked them."

He gave a tight smile. "I'm glad you showed her around. Now, I'm going to head out. Do you need anything?"

He met Cassie's gaze again. It was a kick in the ribs. "No, I think we're fine. I have your number if I need you."

"Then we're all set. Polly is very outspoken and will fill you in on anything you need to know or what she likes to do. Again, thank you for standing in for Erin and your mom. I really appreciate it."

Her pulsed hummed erratically. "I'm glad to help."

He came around the counter. "Polly, I need to talk to Cassie before I leave, so give me my hug and I'll see you in the morning." He leaned down and hugged his little girl. "I love you, pumpkin. You have a good night."

Cassie watched the heartwarming exchange. He kissed the top of Polly's head.

"I love you too, Daddy. I hope you sleep good and no fires."

"I'll be safe even if there is one. I'll see you in the morning, brave girl."

It hit her in that moment that Polly was worried about her daddy but trying not to show it. She'd lost her mother already and her daddy had a job that was dangerous and she knew this. Erin had said Polly was older than her years and now Cassie understood where that came from.

Hunter kissed Polly's head once more, then headed toward the door, and she followed him. He held the door for her; she passed by him and out onto the front porch. She turned when she reached the sidewalk, needing the space of the front yard instead of the small front porch of the bungalow.

"Thanks again for doing this." He came to stand

on the sidewalk too.

"I'm glad to help. Is there anything I need to know before you go?"

He looked thoughtful for a moment and she waited. "Yeah, actually, there is. She's better but Polly has nightmares still. Not like she did when we first came here. But sometimes they hit her. I never know when but just in case she has one, you need to know. They are usually always the same. It's her worrying that I'm in the water with her mom. She worries that she's lost both of us. Therapy is helping, thank God. But I'll be glad of the day she never has another one."

Her heart ached for him and for Polly. "I'm so sorry for what you and Polly have been through. For the loss of your wife. She was beautiful and it shows in the photos how much she loved you both."

Something in his gaze hardened, then he raked a hand through his hair as if exasperated or something. What was that for?

"Yeah," he said. "She loved Polly. Look, if you need me, I'll be here. Brad is real understanding, so if she has a nightmare and you need me, call my number and I'll be here unless I'm out on an emergency. Oh, and she likes to come by the station each morning when I'm there. I try to have a muffin with her or some eggs and bacon if she's in the mood for it. The kid is hooked on Rosie's muffins and she keeps the firehouse supplied, so there is always an assortment."

Cassie smiled. Her sister-in-law did make the best muffins in the world at her Bake My Day bakery. She'd opened it up and put Sunset Bay on the map. Even had an online business she'd recently started up. "I have to agree. So, I'll bring her by. Any certain time?"

He grinned and sun lines crinkled around his eyes. "She'll let you know. But it's usually around eight or near there. My Polly is an early riser, which at least makes getting her up and ready for school easier."

"I'm an early riser myself, so she speaks my language."

They stared at each other for a long moment.

"Okay, well then, I'll head to work. You've got this?"

She figured by the looks of it she was going to

have to push him to his truck and into the cab so he would leave. "I've got this. Go. I promise I'll take good care of your precious cargo."

He frowned. His gaze flickered with pain or anger, or something. She was starting to get used to seeing that look and more and more curious about which it was.

"That's what she is. She's my life, and I'm grateful you're helping me out."

His lips lifted into a crooked smile, one of gratitude. That was easy to read, unlike the other look.

She watched him walk to his truck and climb inside. He lifted a hand in a wave good-bye and then backed out of the driveway. Relief washed over her as he drove down the street. The man made her nervous.

* * *

Hunter checked his gear after he got to work. His thoughts were on Cassie and Polly. He was relieved to know that Cassie was going to be good for Polly, and they were going to have fun while she was there. But it was going to be a constant irritation to him that he kept thinking about how pretty and how nice Cassie was. The fact that she was stepping in like this when he knew that the incident at work had her on edge spoke volumes to him. Maybe while she was watching Polly, she might share more of what was going on inside that pretty head of hers. She was helping him with Polly, so maybe he could reciprocate and help her out. He had been through a lot, so it was sad to say that he had experience dealing with trauma. For the most part, he'd overcome. There were things he hadn't fully come to grips with, but he was dealing with them as best he could. He'd compartmentalized everything and other than the fact that he had decided to live the rest of his life single, he was happy with the way he had decided to handle his future.

Why he kept thinking about Cassie in this way he wasn't sure, but something was eating at her. He'd glimpsed it that night as he'd approached her on the beach. There was more to her story than she'd told him. It bothered him and if he could help her, he would. He set his goal; he liked goals—they gave him something to focus on. And instead of focusing on the fact that she was pretty and interesting and in any other life he would have very much wanted to get to know her better, he would now focus on the fact that she had a problem and he might be able to help her. Even if it was to be a sounding board. Yeah, that was a good goal. It would keep his mind off other things.

"Hey, Hunter, how was your weekend?" Dex Carpenter walked into the locker-room. He set his gear down across from Hunter and opened his locker.

"Hey, Dex." He and Dex got along well. They'd been working together ever since Hunter had moved to town for the job. He was from Sunset Bay and had grown up with all the Sinclairs and most of the crew. He'd never been married and seemed pretty content to stay that way. Hunter had heard rumors that Dex was in love with Cassie. That they went way back. "I had a good weekend. How about yourself? We missed you at the wedding."

Dex hung his duffel bag inside his locker. "I had to go see my sister. I hear it was a good wedding."

"It was. It was a fun time."

Their conversation was stilted. Not as easygoing as usual. In all honesty, Hunter wasn't sure whether it was him or Dex. He had that niggling thought in the back of his mind about Dex and Cassie, wondering what had happened between them. It was something he wasn't going to ask about. As a guy, he didn't dig into other people's business.

Dex closed his locker. "I heard that Cassie is in town. I thought she might be for the wedding. I went by the bakery for a breakfast smoothie and oh you know, Lila and Doreen and that little ladies group were down there, and they said she was watching Polly for you while Erin and Summer are out of town. Is that true?"

So there it was. It wasn't him who was being stilted; it was Dex. There was no way getting around that Dex Carpenter was still fixed on Cassie. Hunter could hear it in his voice and see it in his eyes.

"Yeah, turned out that yesterday I learned that Erin was going on tour with Nash, so Cassie stepped in. She's kind of saving my bacon."

"Is she going to bring Polly by in the morning like

Summer normally does?"

"I think so. I leave it up to Polly to decide if she wants to come by. She's old enough to decide what she wants to do in that respect."

Dex contemplated that for a moment, then nodded and cocked his head toward the mess hall. "I'm on cook duty. I guess I better get in there."

Hunter watched him walk away. He wanted to call out and tell him to relax, that there was nothing between him and Cassie, if that was what was on his mind. But he didn't. The man definitely had something on his mind. Or maybe it went deeper than that. Maybe he needed to ask someone about the situation.

He was on duty to wash the fire engines. Keeping busy was easy at the fire station and he liked that. He did not like sitting around, waiting for a fire to happen or some other emergency. And at home, he was the same way; staying busy was a good thing. Gave him less time to dwell on things he couldn't control or fix.

He headed outside and climbed into the fire truck, and moved it out in front of the station. Several of the other men were on duty, too, and they all got busy scrubbing. Thankfully, Sunset Bay wasn't a terribly busy area and fires weren't an everyday thing, or even an every week thing. But they did get called out to the highway for wrecks. They'd had a few big fires and near misses, but they were highly trained. And when emergencies did happen, they knew what they were doing.

Considering he was Polly's only living relative, he'd decided a small, quaint town on the beach was a good place to raise his daughter. She had enough fears about him drowning or burning in a building. He had to find a way to ease her worries.

Brad walked out of the building. "Hunter, when you get through, I'd like to see you in my office."

"Sure thing, Chief. Let me finish this fender and I'll be right there. Unless you need me this instant."

"Nope, finish what you're doing."

Hunter knew if it had been something major, Brad would have told him to come immediately. After making one more swipe, he handed the rag to the rookie working next to him. "Make sure she sparkles."

He grinned. "I'll make sure of it."

Hunter liked the younger man. Zack had joined up recently—after Hunter had arrived—fresh out of the academy; he had more to learn but he was willing and that was important.

Hunter went inside the building, hung a left and poked his head inside the open doorway. "You ready for me?"

"Come on in. Close the door behind you." Brad stopped typing on the computer, leaned back in his seat and studied him.

"Something wrong?"

"I hear Erin and Mom pulled a big one on you and that Cassie is watching Polly?"

"Yeah, she is. She was a real trouper, stepping in for Erin and your mom so they could go on their trips. I really appreciate her."

"She's all about that. She always steps in when she can, but she has her own life and she's pretty busy. I have to say that Mom and Erin would like if she came home. They always worry about her out there traipsing around by her lonesome. She and I have always been so different. She's like Tate. Me—I've always been content to stay here in Sunset Bay and enjoy the beach life but she and Tate, man, there is just something about throwing themselves off things and diving under things, diving with sharks and such. Or hanging off cliffs or climbing up them. Me, I don't mind climbing into a burning building but I am not hanging off the side of a mountain by a little clip and a rope." He laughed.

Hunter thought about what Cassie had told him about her fall and knew that Brad would not be happy if he knew what had happened to Cassie. "I'm not into that either. It's funny what some call risky, others don't."

"Yeah, but hey, to each his own. Anyway, I just thought I'd warn you about Dex. He's in love with my sister. He's never gotten over the fact that she never loved him back. Dex is a great guy and he does get a little uptight when Cassie is in town. It's not always good when the woman you love doesn't reciprocate. Makes hometown visits rough. He can avoid her usually but if she's bringing Polly to the station in the morning like Summer normally does, then I thought

I'd warn you. He gets a little tense when she's around."

What in the heck was that about? "What do you mean by tense? The guy's not moving on?"

"Not so far. It's like he's stuck on her. Cassie never led him on and just liked him as a friend. But Mom and Erin pushed that, and he thought if he hung on long enough, he could talk her into loving him. But he was never more than a close friend to her. I figure they probably had a kiss or two, with her deciding it wasn't going anywhere—you know when there are sparks and she obviously had none. He, on the other hand, fell madly in love. I'm hoping one day someone will come to town and knock him off his feet. It'd be good for him. But I wanted to warn you so you'd know, there is a little bit of a strain between them."

"Why do I need to know this?" This was getting deeper than he wanted to go.

"I'm just warning you because I saw you at the wedding the other night dancing and then you went out to the beach. I'm thinking he's going to see you two together and he's going to think there is something between you two. He needs to get over her anyway because nothing is ever going to happen between them. I feel his pain. I was a little bit in his shoes there for a long time, and Lulu coming to town was the best thing that ever happened to me. He's not to that point after all this time and I'm starting to feel bad for the guy.

"Truth is, him seeing you two and thinking there is something between you two might be good for him. He might be able to move on and not linger on something that's never going to happen. Cassie is never going to love him. So, I'm just warning you—telling you that if by some chance there is something brewing between you and my sister, I'm all for it. But I need to warn you that her heart is out there…somewhere in that craziness she craves. But I like the guy and maybe it would be doing him a favor, maybe if he believed there was something between you and Cassie. Maybe he could move on."

He stared at his boss. Not totally sure what he was thinking he'd just heard and what had actually just been said were the same things. "Hold on, let me clarify because I'm really confused right now. Are you telling me that you want me to make Dex think there is something between me and Cassie, or are you telling me that you would like there to be something between me and Cassie?"

Brad grinned a big, lazy smile and relaxed in his leather chair. "Either of the above. Or all of the above. I'm easy—I'm good. I can't deny that I would be fine if my sister decided to stop hanging off the side of mountains and bridges and came home to settle down. We miss her. And Tate, you know he has a life here now. Maybe Cassie could find that. And you've been here months now and haven't gone out on a single date. I'm thinking that while she's hanging out with you and Polly that you could ask her out on a date."

The room seemed uncomfortably hotter suddenly. "Brad, I'm…you know my wife messed around on me. You know that. No one else knows about it, but you do. I'm pretty sure I'm not going to start dating again. I'm not planning on ever getting married again." He had been certain he wasn't and now he's saying he was pretty sure he wasn't. What was that about? "It wouldn't be fair to Cassie for me to date her when I have no intention of ever marrying again."

Brad looked incredulous. "Hunter, your wife obviously had some kind of problem and your entire world was shaken to the core in a matter of twenty-four hours. But, man, you can't say never. Look at all the years you could be here, growing old alone. Look at Polly. She needs a mom."

"We're doing fine." He gritted the words out.

Brad held his hands up. "Fine. You're doing fine. I just wanted to throw that out there. Just in case you decided to toss these depressing notions out you have about your life and that you decide to start fresh and think about a bright, new future. If that were to happen, you have my blessing. I think you and my sister would get along."

Hunter willed his temper to recede. Brad was just trying to be a friend. "Look, I get your message. Now I'm going to go start washing the next fire truck."

Brad nodded. "Sounds like a plan. My sweet wife, Lulu, will be very glad we had this talk. She was about to bug me to death last night wanting me to let you know that you have our blessing. I can tell you there is a whole Sinclair clan out there with their eyes on you."

He stood. Perfect. Just perfect. Not only did he have a whole bunch of folks wishing him and Cassie would get together, but his boss was also hoping he'd at least fake it to help a poor fellow firefighter move on with his life. What a whole bunch of mixed-up craziness was going on here. "I hope everyone isn't going to get upset with me. I am just treading water trying to make a life for Polly."

"I get it, man, just keep an open mind."

Hunter nodded, probably grimmer than Brad was expecting but this was not pressure he wanted. Nothing else to say, he headed back outside, shaking his head and wondering whether he had awakened in another dimension or something because his life had just taken an unreal turn.

CHAPTER SIX

Polly asked Cassie to read to her before she went to sleep. Cassie enjoyed spending time with the sweet little girl. They decided to make chicken spaghetti for dinner—a favorite of both of theirs, they found out. They worked together in the kitchen. Polly stood on a stool and carefully placed noodles in the boiling water. Cassie stood beside her, hovering to make sure the six-year-old didn't get too close to the pot that was on the back burner, as far away from her as Cassie could get it.

"You can relax. I watch the little kids on the food

cooking shows work near the oven and stove all the time and they don't get hurt much."

Cassie cringed, thinking about it. "It's the 'much' part that I'm nervous about. I'm sure they are being watched carefully. That's why I will stay right here beside you, just in case. Even adults have accidents." The moment the words were out of her mouth, she wanted to snatch them back. If anyone knew that accidents happened, it would be this little girl. But Polly didn't act as if she caught what Cassie had said, thank goodness.

"I know, but I really can do this. But thanks for caring."

That took her by surprise. She did sound like a little adult. "I do care. And I'm so glad I get to spend time with you. My mother going on a cruise and Erin going on a book tour and then Summer going on a honeymoon did me a favor because I get to spend time with you. And I'm not used to spending time with little girls. Did you know that?"

Polly giggled as she placed the last of the spaghetti in the pot. "I know. Aunt Summer told me that I was going to have to teach you how to be around little girls. But she said we would have a lot in common because I like to explore and she said you are an explorer because you do all kinds of cool things with your job."

"Well now, I never thought of myself as an explorer, but I do like the sound of it. And I do like adventures."

"Me too. Do you think after we go see my daddy in the morning that we can go on an adventure? Maybe we can go do a picnic and watch for manatees. Or we can go to the lookout and watch for porpoises."

"Sure, we can do that. Are we going to see your daddy in the morning?" This last question she asked hesitantly.

Polly looked sheepish. "Yes. I like to see my daddy in the morning and get a hug from him."

Cassie smiled. "I like to get hugs from my mom and dad, too, and I'm a lot older than you are. I'm sure your daddy wants a hug from you."

"And he needs them. He told me he needs them a lot."

"I'm sure he does." She thought about that statement for a long while as they ate dinner and then did some coloring in a coloring book, and she mulled it over as Polly took her bath and then climbed into bed. This little family needed a lot of love. They had both been hurt so much, not just Polly but Hunter too. She could only imagine how much he did need hugs from his little girl. He'd told her Polly was his joy and his life. He was most likely still hurting deeply.

She was tucking Polly's covers in around her when she settled back on her pillows and looked at Cassie with sleepy eyes. Cassie wanted to hug her.

"Daddy usually reads to me. Will you read to me?"

"Sure. What do you want me to read?"

Polly picked a book off the windowsill. "I like this one. It's one of the ones my mama gave me before she died. I have others I like to read but tonight I want to hear this one. It's a really good book and you'll enjoy it too."

Cassie's heart clutched. She felt completely inadequate reading Sandra Claremont's little girl a bedtime story that the woman had obviously wanted to read to her baby herself. The weight of it hit heavy. Her throat tightened as she took it from Polly. "I would be happy to read it to you. Your mother must have loved it very much to give it to you. I'm certain you were her little princess."

Polly snuggled into the pillow. Her dark curls fanned out about her face in a halo. "She did. She called me her little princess. We really liked doing the same things. I hope one day I get to go boating and fishing more. You know, my mama was a fisherwoman. She did it professionally."

"I had suspected as much from the pictures. There are a lot of pictures of you and her fishing."

Polly nodded and looked around the room. "She liked sport fishing. Do you know what that means? They catch them and let them go."

"I did know that, but I think it's great that you know so much about it. She and your daddy taught you well."

"I want to be as good as her one day."

Cassie gently pushed a lock of hair away from her

eye. "From the looks of these pictures, you will do that."

Polly toyed with the book. "Maybe. I have to be able to get back in the water. I have nightmares, I bet my daddy told you. I have nightmares about the water. I got to get on the water with Jonah and Summer once. And we saved a man who was drowning. I didn't get scared or worried right then but later I had nightmares again. And they make my daddy really sad. My doctor told me that I'll know when it's okay for me to be on the water again. My mama loved it and I did too, and I want to do it again."

She sniffed and Cassie did too. She couldn't move. What could she say?

This was so much more than she'd anticipated.

"Polly, I believe that you'll do it too. You and your daddy will know when it's right. But if you want something bad enough, you can achieve anything. You just have to do it little by little sometimes. Including overcoming these nightmares that you have. And I can only believe that your daddy will help you in any way he can. He wants you to succeed. It's only natural for him to worry about you. Now, let's relax and read this lovely book from your mama. In the morning, we'll go see your daddy and then go on a great adventure together."

Polly nodded, and as Cassie leaned back against the headboard and opened the book, Polly leaned her soft head against her arm and snuggled there while Cassie read. "There once was a delightful tiny fairy…"

Moments later, with only a few pages read, Polly was sound asleep. Cassie was wide awake and sat on the bed with Polly's head snuggled against her arm. Cassie sat like that for a very long time, feeling off-balance and out of her element.

And her thoughts shifted from Hunter's sweet child and the trauma she'd been through to him. He was a man with a lot on his shoulders. And her heart ached for him and Polly.

* * *

"So you made it okay last night, pumpkin?" Hunter asked the next morning after Polly and Cassie had arrived at the fire station. They sat outside at a picnic table on the side of the building.

"I did, Daddy. Aunt Cassie and me had a great time. We cooked dinner, I helped, and then she read to me out of one of Mama's books and she stayed with me until I fell asleep. This morning, she was awake before I was. I didn't have to wake her up like I have to do to you sometimes."

He laughed, relieved that it had all gone so well. Cassie laughed, too, and their gazes met. She looked beautiful this morning. Her wavy hair was pulled back at the nape of her neck and tendrils had escaped about her face. She looked rested and fresh, and he could have sat and looked at her for hours. But it was the life and compassion in her eyes that drew him to her. Made him want to know more.

He'd had her on his mind all night and hoped they'd made it okay. Polly's happiness proved that all had gone better than even he had hoped.

"Hey," he said in response to Polly's teasing. "I sleep late sometimes because I've had a rough night."

His daughter scrunched her cute face up as she

paused eating the strawberry cream cheese delight muffin she was tearing into from Bake My Day. "I know. Sometimes you don't sleep at night and you roam around the house."

It was true; he had insomnia a lot of the time and he did tend to wander around, unable to lay in bed and remain there. "Enough about my bad sleeping habits. Tell me about the adventures you two planned for today. It's a beautiful day and you need to take advantage of them before you have to return to school...gee, that's only a week away." Polly was munching madly on her muffin now, so he looked at Cassie as the cool morning wind buffeted the tendrils about her face. He hitched an eyebrow at her. "You might as well fill me in because the little one is clearly focused on her muffin now."

"I don't blame her." Cassie smiled as she pulled the wrapper away from her own muffin. "We're going to take a picnic lunch, that we're picking up at Bake My Day. Rosie is putting it together and we're both eager to see what she puts in the basket. That's the first adventure, after seeing you, of course." She smiled and

Polly gave an enthusiastic thumbs-up as she took another bite of her muffin. "Then we're going up to the lookout point and watch for porpoises. After that, we're going to go down and walk the beach and see what we can spot—stingrays swimming on the waves, or sea turtles or conch shells. It will be an adventure to see what shows up."

"I'm impressed. Sounds like a great adventure, exactly like something Polly would love."

Cassie studied him, her eyes warm and so distracting that he stopped talking.

"That's what she told me but I wanted to make sure it was all okay with you."

"I think it's a great idea. My only regret is that I can't come too. But I have to stay here."

Polly suddenly swallowed hard. "Daddy, maybe when you get off from your shift we can go on the boat and Cassie can come with us. You promised we would go before I went back to school." Polly looked at him with an expectant expression. "You promised."

Ah, yes, he had promised. He sighed silently, knowing the time was here. He was going to have to do what he had promised and had been putting off.

Cassie looked at Polly then him, clearly curious at what he was going to say. Maybe, because he was a big chicken, Cassie coming along might be a good thing. She could be helpful, maybe a buffer. His eyes narrowed with the magnitude of the whole idea of him taking his daughter out on a boat for the first time since the accident. What if she grew terrified he was going to die once they were out there? He would have to drive the boat to get her back. Extra arms to comfort his daughter would be a good thing.

"Would you mind coming? I know it would be your day off, but I did promise her and..." He struggled with how to put this with Polly sitting right there. He rubbed his hand on the varnished wooden top of the picnic table. She seemed to look into his very soul in that moment and gave him the most understanding smile. It made him feel as if she could read every shaky thought he was having.

"If you two want me to go, I would love to. Polly has told me how excited she is to try it but also how hard it could be for both of you."

He looked at Polly, his wise and wonderful, sweet girl.

"It's true, Daddy. You know that you are having a hard time taking me out on the water and I know it could be scary. For both of us. But maybe with Aunt Cassie being along, we can be braver. And we can show her how good you can drive a boat and maybe I can drive one again. I barely remember driving it if I don't look at the pictures with me and Mam..." Sadness flickered in her eyes as her voice trailed off. Then she smiled. "Like I used to do when Mama was with us."

How had he been blessed with such an extraordinary brave and sweet little girl? She was an inspiration to him for her courage. "Then we're going to plan it. I get off in two days. Then we will give Cassie time to go home to sleep in her own bed and relax for a few hours, then we'll go. How does that sound?"

"I think that would be a perfect idea. It will give you a night to rest and then we'll go. It will be a fun day. We'll knock this fear out of the way. I've found in my own life that if I'm afraid of something, if I just jump back in there—although I've never had anything of the magnitude of what you two have been through—but for myself, tackling something I'm a little worried about always works best if I take it by the horns and just do it."

Polly reached out and laid her tiny hand on top of Cassie's as she looked with complete trust at this woman who she'd just come to know. "I like you, Aunt Cassie. I like how brave you are."

Cassie swallowed hard and he realized that her suddenly bright eyes were signaling tears. Her voice cracked slightly. "No, Polly, you are the brave one. I admire you with all my heart and I know your mama does too. She's going to be watching you from heaven and will be so proud of you pushing forward."

He watched his little girl straighten her shoulders as she looked at Cassie with the sweetest look on her face. His heart clenched hard.

"I think so, too," Polly said. "She wants me to do this. She likes you, too. I feel it."

Cassie's gaze lifted to his and there was empathy in those beautiful eyes of hers. She had no clue about everything that had transpired before that accident, but the one thing she did know was that his baby needed special love.

Even though she was being brave, he knew she was still vulnerable. But...she was trying to face her fears and that was more than he was doing.

Cassie was so good with Polly that it made him wonder whether he was being fair to his daughter by letting the past failure of his marriage keep him from trying again.

Until now, until Cassie, he hadn't questioned his decision to not trust—no, he hadn't questioned his fear of trusting another woman...

His thoughts were interrupted as he saw Dex emerge from the station house and start their way. He shifted his thoughts but knew he was going to go back and look at them more closely. It was time.

He saw Cassie's attention had also gone to the approaching fireman.

* * *

Cassie tensed as she saw Dex come out of the fire

station and cross the grass toward them. Hunter saw him, too, and his gaze skipped back to hers, searching. She wondered whether he had heard about the history she shared with Dex.

"Hey, Cassie." Dex smiled at her and nodded at Hunter and Polly.

"Hi, Dex." Polly grinned at him.

Cassie had wondered whether he was on duty and whether she would see her old friend. "Dex. How are you?" She got up and gave him a quick hug. They'd been friends for so long and she hated with all of her heart that Dex had wanted more from their friendship than she had been able to give him. He was a wonderful man but just not the man for her.

"I'm good. Can we talk for a minute?"

"Sure. I'll be right back," she said to Hunter and Polly, and then walked with Dex out toward the sidewalk near the flagpole.

"I heard you were going to be in town for a little while. I was wondering if you might want to go out sometime?"

"I'm not sure that's a good idea." She hesitated.

They had been friends and they'd been avoiding each other when she was in town. It was very awkward, like now, when they were in the same room or area together.

"It's been a while since we spent any time together and I thought we could…for old time's sake, go out for dinner or coffee…whatever works for you." He held her gaze with steady eyes.

Her heart tugged with the friendship they'd shared for so long. It seemed wrong to just shut him out without seeing whether they could find that friendship again without the awkwardness his falling in love with her had caused. "I think that would be nice. It's been a long time. It will be nice to catch up."

He looked pleased. "Great. How about tonight?"

"I'm keeping Polly until Hunter's shift is over in two days."

"Then we're in luck. That's when my shift ends too." He smiled. "What about Saturday evening, the day after you get off?"

He had always had such a great smile. "I'm going out on the boat with Hunter and Polly that morning, but the evening should be fine."

"You're going with Hunter?"

"Yes, and Polly. Anyway, I better get back to them. I'll see you later."

"Yeah, sure. How about seven on Saturday?"

She smiled at him. "Yes. I'll be ready. I'm staying at my mom and dad's."

"Just like the old days." He leaned forward and hugged her.

Startled, she laid her hands lightly on his shoulders, then stepped back. He was strong and handsome, and a really nice guy. But she had no butterflies before and there none now. But she was going to have an open mind.

CHAPTER SEVEN

After seeing Hunter at the fire station, Cassie and Polly went back home for a couple of hours and then they headed up to Bake My Day. Cassie couldn't stop thinking about Hunter and Polly. There was a connection between them that mystified her. She had known Dex for most of her life and yet it was Hunter, whom she barely knew, she felt as if she'd always known.

He was so worried about his daughter. How could she not go on the boat with them?

She was glad to be here; it felt like this was where

she was supposed to be. Cassie wanted to be there as support for Polly—and for Hunter—on Saturday when they went out on the boat.

When they entered the bakery, the cool breeze followed them through the door and everyone turned to see who had entered with the wind. There were a lot of familiar faces.

"Polly Claremont, you little cutie pie...come see us," Mami Desmond exclaimed from the corner table where she sat with her friends, Lila, Doreen, and Birdie. "Cassie, you come on over, too. We've been wanting to talk to you."

Lila looked excited to see her, and Cassie knew the older woman wanted to know whether there was anything romantic going on between her and Hunter.

"Come on," she called, patting the chair beside her.

Cassie had never been happier to have plans than she was right in that moment. "I need to check on our picnic basket with Rosie. But I'll be there in a minute." At least that bought her a couple of minutes.

"We'll be here," Birdie grunted. "I saw you two

sitting at the firehouse picnic table this morning when I drove by. I honked and hollered, and I'd have waved but y'all were so deep in conversation you didn't even hear me."

"You honked? And I didn't hear you?"

"Well, I sort of honked. My old horn doesn't work too well and it just tooted like a weak toy horn. But I hollered really loud."

She hadn't heard that? "I'm sorry I didn't hear you." They really had been deep in conversation, no denying it. But she had no intention of talking about any of her conversation with Hunter with these four ladies. Not unless she wanted everyone in town to know details that were so personal to Hunter and Polly.

"It's okay. You and Hunter talking is a good thing. Sharing time with my little buddy here." Birdie grinned at Polly, who immediately hugged the tiny woman.

"We're going on a boat, Miss Birdie."

"Oh, are you now. Well, it is about time."

Polly grinned. "Aunt Cassie is going too."

"And that's a great idea."

"It certainly is," Mami declared, looking as if she'd just been awarded the Publishers Clearing House Award. "It's simply delightful."

"It really is," Lila agreed, clapping her hands together and smiling broadly.

"Oh, sweetie, I'm so excited for you. I know how much you've been wanting to go out again." Doreen smiled shyly.

"I'm so excited." Polly engulfed the shy woman.

Doreen looked so pleased as she hugged Polly. "You are just about the sweetest girl I know."

Polly leaned back and looked very seriously at her. "You are the sweetest lady. And you're soft and fluffy too."

Everyone chuckled because Doreen was very well endowed.

Cassie chuckled, too, and took that moment of distraction to head toward the counter.

"Hi, lucky girl," Gigi said softly and leaned forward over the counter to get closer. She quirked her finger at Cassie.

Cassie leaned closer and whispered, "What are

you talking about?"

"You are spending time with Hunter, aren't you?"

"Yes. But, it's not like that and you know it," she hissed.

Gigi laughed. "Yeah, right. I think you two make a great couple."

"Seriously, there is nothing between us."

Gigi frowned. "Then make something happen."

"I'm not going to do that."

"Well, I'm thinking that is a mistake. Just so you know." Gigi gave her a you-know-what-I'm talking-about look and moved toward the coffee machine.

Rosie moved carefully from the back room, her sweet face fuller because she was so far along with the pregnancy. "I've got the special picnic ready."

"Thank you. How are you feeling?"

"I'm so ready to meet my baby. I'm not really working much but for a few hours split into shifts of sitting and standing. In other words, a lot of breaks." She smiled and radiated happiness. "I'm happy I'm able to help out some. I need to be here because I'm going mad at home, twiddling my thumbs."

"Believe me, I would be too. But then I was surprised to be watching Polly, but it's actually been a good thing. We're having fun and over the next few weeks, it will help me not get bored."

Better to say that than tell anyone she believed she was meant to be here helping Hunter with Polly. That would sound so farfetched. She didn't understand it herself, but it just felt right.

However, if she said anything about her feelings, it might start talk that there was something between them or that she wanted something to be between them, and she didn't.

Are you sure?

"You'll do great with Polly," Rosie said softly. "I think you coming home is meant to be."

Cassie's breath caught and her heartbeat quickened. "What did you say?"

"You heard me. I think you and Hunter are meant to be." Rosie slid the picnic basket forward, looking as though she knew a secret.

Cassie slowly exhaled as she took the basket. "Rosie, don't read more into this than there is. I'm just helping out."

"I know and it's because you have a good heart. And that is exactly what Hunter and Polly both need."

Panic welled inside her. "N-no, do not get carried away, Rosie." She leaned closer. "And please do not tell them." She rolled her eyes toward Lila and her friends as they talked happily with Polly about the adventure they were about to go on. "That won't do anyone any good."

"I won't. I'm just telling you what I feel. When you were home last time, I saw you and I saw Hunter, and I just got this warm, fuzzy feeling about the two of you."

She felt really uncomfortable with this conversation. Despite her own feelings that she was here for a reason, this felt too cozy. Too confining, because Rosie saw them as a couple and she just felt right being here. There was a huge difference. "Rosie, I'm just hoping I don't do them any harm."

"You won't. Just be yourself. Now, you and Polly have a great time."

Gigi came over and slid a paper cup of coffee

toward her. "Here, this is our new blend, caramel mocha with a twist. Enjoy." Gigi smiled widely. "Tate and I would love for you to come out to the house and see what he's doing with the stunt man school. Maybe bring Polly out and her good-looking daddy, too. It'll be fun."

"Tell my brother I'm coming out there and that I want to fall off a tall platform onto one of those big pillows. And by the way, I'm so happy you two are together."

Gigi smiled. "Me too."

"Now, I have a date with the cutest little six-year-old in town."

* * *

The day Hunter got off, he walked into the house and found Polly sitting in Cassie's lap. They were reading a book. Cassie smiled at him, and Polly jumped up and raced across the room.

"Daddy, you're home." She threw herself at him and he caught her up in his arms and hugged her tight.

His gaze connected with Cassie's as she watched them, looking happy.

"How are you, pumpkin?"

Polly leaned back and took his face in her hands. "I'm great. Aunt Cassie has been reading a lot of stories with me. I'm glad you're home."

"I'm glad to be here. How are you, Cassie?"

"I'm great. We've had fun." She smiled at him. "It looks like my duty here is done. I'm going to leave you two so you can have a few days together."

Polly scrambled out of his arms and rushed to her, throwing her arms around her legs and squeezing. "I have loved you being here. Are you coming tomorrow?"

Cassie ran her hand over Polly's hair and looked down at her upturned face. "I wouldn't miss it for the world."

"Great," Polly said with delight.

Hunter's heart ached at the picture they made, standing like that and then of them on the couch, snuggled up, reading. Things a mother would do.

"I'll see you then." Cassie bent down and hugged

his daughter, then headed toward the door, where her things were waiting.

"Polly, I'm going to walk Cassie to the car. I'll be right back."

"I'm going to get my dolls ready for a tea party. Will you come have tea with us?"

"I'll be there as soon as I come back inside."

He hurried to take the bag from Cassie's shoulder. Their fingers brushed and a heat of awareness sliced through him. He smiled. "I'll take this."

She let him and then walked out onto the porch after he opened the door. "A tea party. You're a good daddy, Hunter Claremont." She smiled as she walked down the steps and he moved to walk beside her.

"I try. You know, to do the things a mom would do, too."

"She did well. I know you said she has nightmares and they come out of nowhere but she slept really well. She misses you. But that's normal for kids to want to see their parents."

"Maybe I worry too much. Maybe I'm the needy one?" He placed her bag in the backseat.

"I'm no expert but I think all parents worry. You have an extra burden and a total right to worry. You're not needy—just concerned. Your job makes it more difficult too, but then you have the days off grouped together, so that makes up for the days away. And then breakfast like you do." She laid a hand on his arm. "I think you're doing amazing."

Her words touched him, and he liked that she thought so. He worried about it a lot. He looked down at the ground, thoughts rolling. He tucked his fingers into his pockets then looked at her. "I need to explain a few things before we get on the water tomorrow."

She leaned back against her SUV, as if to give him all the time he needed. "I thought as much."

"Cassie, Polly has parts of her memory pertaining to the accident that she doesn't remember. That's part of why I'm worried about the trip. When she went with Jonah and Summer, nothing really came to the surface. But with me on the boat, I don't know...with the nightmares she has and her worries—that she is trying hard not to have or to show..." He paused. "Who knows, maybe it's just me thinking she's worried and she really isn't. I hope that's the case and that she is doing as good as she acts."

"I know you're worried, and I completely understand your fear now that I know she has memory blocks."

He took a deep breath. "No one knows what happened in the moments that led to an experienced boater running her boat head on into a rock jetty. The only person who could have any insight into that is Polly, but she has no memory of those moments."

"Wow, I didn't know. I understand now. I promise to be there and it helps knowing this."

Her eyes were so beautiful and full of compassion. Cassie the adventurer was a good person. He struggled with the urge to pull her into his arms and see whether she would come. He saw flickers of awareness in her eyes, too, at times, especially when they touched…but instead, he stepped back.

"Thanks for being so good to Polly. Go enjoy your day." He crossed his arms to keep them where they should be—not hugging Cassie. He had seen her and Dex hug, and during their shift, Dex had said she was going out with him. Not that it mattered to him, he reminded himself, but she and Dex had a history together and her time here might be the thing that moved it to the here and now. He needed to keep his head on straight.

Instead of getting in her car, she hesitated and bit her lip, as if holding back more she might want to say. He stood still and waited, but with a tight smile, she got into her car. It felt like much was left unsaid, hanging in the air, and he knew for him it was the accident. He still hadn't told her everything.

Moments later, she gave a small wave as she drove away and left him watching her SUV disappear down the lane. He finally inhaled, then slowly expelled it and tried to calm his racing heart. Something was going on that he hadn't felt in a very long time. It wasn't something he wanted to feel, but now... He turned and went back into the house. His thoughts were spinning out of control.

It was time for a tea party and a big bright smile from the light of his life.

* * *

Cassie drove away and watched Hunter in her rearview. He stood there, straight and tall, with his muscled arms crossed over his chest, as he watched her drive away. He looked to her like a man with the world on his shoulders. It was a hard thing to bear, she was sure, the worry that he carried. She had not known that Polly had a blocked memory. Poor kid. But it was understandable—those moments of the crash had to have been horrific. The very idea that she might remember them while on a boat ride with her and Hunter made her worry that she would be so inadequate in the situation. Really, what did she know about a child?

Panic seized her just as her phone rang. She was walking into her mom's home. A glance at the phone, after she fished it from her back pocket, showed Erin's face. She tapped the screen and her sister's smiling face lifted her spirits.

"Hey, sis. I was just checking in on you. I know you're just getting off."

Cassie smiled, and the panic eased some. "You are right on the spot. I'm just walking in the door. How's the book tour?"

"It's amazing. I can't thank you enough for taking my spot and enabling me to come with Nash. We'll be in Paris together, so romantic, and it's all because of you."

"Enough already with the thanks. I'm glad you're having a wonderful time."

Erin dipped her chin. "Are you?" she cooed. "How are you?"

"I'm…okay, so I'm fine to a point. Polly is awesome. What a great kid. Such a sweetheart. I would do just about anything for that little girl now."

"She is a darling. And so brave. And I just knew you and her would be buddies. See, her mom, from what Summer tells me, loved being active and pushing for her dreams. Hunter is the same in many ways, and I just thought Polly might be made of the same stuff. She seems like it to me. Anyway, how about things between you and Hunter?"

She did not miss the eagerness of Erin's question.

Cassie took a breath. Her hand still felt a warm tingle from when she grabbed Hunter's arm—when she'd meant to comfort him and had waylaid her senses by touching him. What a bad move on her part. Keep her hands to herself was her new motto.

"We're getting along. He is such a good daddy and so concerned. Erin, do not tell a soul this, but did you know that Polly has no memory of the moments of the accident? The poor child can't remember what happened and that means Hunter doesn't know what happened to his baby or his wife or why she, being an experienced boater, ran that boat full-throttle into that rock jetty. It's horrible."

Erin's expression went slack. "No. I-I didn't know that. I think I would have known that, unless he's keeping it silent. If that's his wish, then that's why Summer wouldn't have said anything."

"I think you're right. And, after he told me this information moments ago before I left, I'm thinking there's something he isn't telling me. I don't know why I feel that way, except he looked almost as if he started to say something more and stopped himself."

"Wow, it just keeps getting worse and worse."

They stared at each other, and Cassie was thankful for video calling because she drew some comfort in her sister at least sharing her same impressions about the situation. "I'm sorry if he doesn't want anyone else to know this, but I was shocked and, frankly, starting to panic right when you called."

Erin's brows dipped. "Wait, why did he share this with you? It's a good sign that you're bonding."

"Over Polly, maybe so. He shared it because I'm going out on a boat with them tomorrow. It's his and Polly's first trip since the accident and the poor guy is terrified. He shared the reason for his concern so I would know the details in case Polly has an episode. You know, remembers and gets emotional. Erin, I'm not equipped for this. What if she does? Who am I to be able to comfort her or know what to say?"

Erin's shoulders relaxed and her head tilted as her eyes softened with compassion for her. "Don't sell yourself short. There is so much to you, sister. You are a woman of determination and deep understanding of what people need. You don't just hang off the sides of mountains and hike to remote places for shots of the most unique and crazy, in my mind, wedding photos. Yes, you do more than wedding photos in crazy places that you couldn't pay me to get near, but it's the wedding photos or anniversary photos that you do that come from a need inside of you to make people happy. You, my sweet sister, do whatever it takes to capture special moments in special places for people. You are strong, adventurous, and compassionate. You don't do it for the money, though the money is a nice perk. I believe you would do some of it for the feeling of fulfillment you get from being able to make someone's dream come true."

Cassie was stunned by her sister's words. "I'm speechless."

Erin laughed, her eyes twinkling. "See, I know you. And one thing I know is that you are what Polly needs. And I'm hoping what Hunter needs. You will give them whatever you can of that big, compassionate heart of yours to see them through this."

Cassie's mouth went dry. She would, she realized. It had happened so very quickly. It was as if she had been caught in a vortex revolving around Hunter and

Polly, and she wanted with all of her heart to see them through this uncertain time. The grief was normal, but this explained so much to her about the added layer of complexity that came with it.

"Am I right?"

She nodded. "Yes. But Erin, I may hurt them in the end. I'm going back to my life. I may be the last person Hunter should have confessed this to."

"Let the future worry about itself. That's one of the things I learned with Nash. If your heart gets involved, maybe loosen the reins on it and let it explore. Okay, I've got to run. Love you."

"Love you more. Take care of yourself and that handsome author of yours."

She laughed. "I'm planning on it."

Cassie walked out onto the back deck overlooking the ocean. She wrapped her arms around her and inhaled the salty air. It filled her soul and calmed her some as she let Erin's words seep in. Could she give of herself to Hunter and Polly without losing her heart?

Could she walk away in the end?

Was she in danger of getting in too deep?

CHAPTER EIGHT

On Saturday morning, Cassie met Hunter and Polly at the pier.

As they waved at her from the boat, her heart felt full and as she drew closer, butterflies fluttered in her chest when she saw Hunter's smile. This was so dangerous. She'd had him and Polly on her mind ever since leaving them.

Hunter was dressed in casual blue shorts and a white T-shirt that stretched over his muscled chest. He looked relaxed and fit and completely engaging as she walked toward him. She liked everything about him very, very much. She told herself as she walked toward him not to let her guard down. Despite what Erin had said about her yesterday, Cassie had reminded herself that she was here only for a short while to get her own life figured out, and these were two wounded souls who did not need her uncertain heart messing them up anymore. Until she understood whether she was truly ready to think about settling down, or whether the fall had simply mixed her up and she would be back to normal soon, she needed to get the thoughts of romance out of her mind. And romance with Hunter had been slipping into her thoughts. This, too, was uncomfortable to her because she knew he might still be mourning his deceased wife.

She was a temporary nanny. Only filling in for these short two weeks and she couldn't forget that for them more than for herself.

"Are you ready for a boat ride?" he asked as she reached them. He held his hand out to her.

"I'm excited about it." She slipped her hand into his and tingles raced up her arm. She'd felt those tingles before but today they were stronger because she knew him better. Knew what kind of man he was, and she admired him very much. It was not because she was falling for the guy she'd only just begun really knowing for a week. She'd known him as a friend of the family who worked with her brother, and seeing him in town briefly only a couple of times when she was home. But she hadn't actually known him, and he was everything a woman could want in a man. What was she thinking?

"I'm so glad you're here!" Polly lunged at her and threw her arms around her.

Instantly, Cassie's heart melted into a pool inside her chest. She was so in trouble. "I'm taking that as you're excited and ready for this."

"I am. I'm going to be brave and I know Daddy is safe like me and Jonah and Summer were when we went out on the water back in the summertime. We're all wearing life vests."

Hunter held hers out to her. "She's right. We're all wearing life vests. Even us experienced boaters." Even though he was smiling, there was strain around his eyes.

Cassie reached for the life vest. "I always wear a life vest. Thank you. And I'm a very experienced boat woman, so I believe with all three of us together, we should have this handled just fine."

"I told Daddy you were perfect because you knew boats."

She loved anything that had to do with sports and being active and having an adventure. Having been raised on the water here in Sunset Bay, boating held a special place in her heart. Just like it held a special place in Polly and also in Hunter's heart...he'd shared his love of boating with his wife.

Remember the wife. The wife he still loved.

The reminder was just what she needed to help get her head back on straight. "Okay, so do we have everything? Can I help untie the boat?"

"Nope, just slip that vest on and sit down with Polly, and I'll get us untied and pushed off and we'll be on our way."

She snapped the vest in place. Polly scampered up onto the bench seat. "Nobody goes without a life jacket, no matter how comfortable you are on the water. It's very dangerous. My mama did not have her life vest on and now she's up in heaven and I don't want you to go there yet." She patted the seat beside her.

Oh, this child hurt her heart. "Believe me, dear, I will wear it always. Now, let's get this show on the road." She met Hunter's gaze and it dug deep straight to her heart, too.

He smiled and to her dismay, though they weren't even touching, tingles swept through her like fireworks bursting in the sky. Whew, this was going to be a long day.

She watched Hunter push the boat away from the dock and then smile as he took the wheel and started the engine. He looked good standing there with the breeze blowing his short, blunt-cut hair. And with a wink their way, he pulled back on the throttle and took them slowly out into the bay. Polly snuggled close and eagerly smiled into the wind. Cassie tightened her arm around the sweet girl and kissed the top of her head.

Despite the battle waging inside her, Cassie knew she wouldn't miss it for the world.

* * *

Hunter had barely slept last night and prayed several times that the day would be good for Polly. She certainly seemed ready. He glanced back and saw her snuggled close to Cassie, with their faces both smiling into the wind and the sunshine. His heart was full, looking at them that way.

Feeling hopeful, he drove the boat out into open water and headed past the mangroves. There were a few other boats out but not any near them. The teal blue called out to him and he wondered whether that was what was helping Polly, too. Once the ocean was a part of you, it was hard to let it go.

A porpoise sprang from the water like a ballerina and Polly squealed in delight. "I love them."

"I do too." Cassie gasped, watching the porpoise as it jumped again and again. "I forgot the way they love to play with boats."

"Yes, they do," he said, smiling at her. Then he spotted the fish. He pointed. "Look ahead—what do you see?" He glanced at them.

Polly leaned her head to the side and stared hard. Her pixie face squeezed in concentration. "Birds. I see them, Daddy."

"And what does that mean?"

"It means the fish are there." She clapped her hands in excitement. "We found the fish!"

He laughed. "Yes, we did. Are you ready to catch a few?"

"I was born ready to catch fish, Daddy." Polly bounced in her seat, her smile as big as the morning sun.

Hunter's heart hurt suddenly watching her and he prayed that he had been wrong and that she was moving forward better than he'd believed. He would move heaven and earth to have her feeling free of any fear and hurt that still lingered from the accident and the loss of her mother.

* * *

Cassie felt her excitement as Hunter tugged on the steering wheel; the boat turned right and headed straight toward the fish. Tension that she'd felt since yesterday eased as the salty air and gorgeous blue water surrounded them. They were going fishing and Polly was excited.

This was not at all what she had been imagining all night long. And for that, she was so thankful.

For the next hour, she watched Polly and her daddy pull one mahi-mahi after the other out of the water. It was amazing. And Polly giggled with every one of them.

"Come on, Aunt Cassie. Come fish," Polly said after a while.

"No, I'm loving watching you two pros go at it. Goodness, y'all are professionals."

Hunter hitched a massive shoulder. "Nah, we just like enjoying it at our own pace. For me, fishing is about relaxing. For a professional, it gets more about the winning."

"My mama was serious when she fished. But I still enjoyed it. But with Daddy, I get so excited and we smile a lot."

The words sank in. Had she sensed a tension in

Hunter in those words? Did he and his Sandra have different views where fishing was concerned? His gaze met hers and held. A shiver raced through her.

"No, I think you've sat long enough. It's time for you to come show us what you've got. And if it's not much, we can help you get better." His smile blossomed and he winked, letting her know he was teasing.

She stood. "I grew up on the water but watching you two makes me think you might be able to…or is it just luck because you happened to park this boat right over the top of a school of mahi?"

"Maybe both?" He grinned and Polly giggled.

She loved hearing the child's giggle, but it was Hunter's smile at that moment that pulled her across the boat to stand near him. "May I take my pick of the rod and reels?"

"Any one you want is fine with me."

She reached behind him and picked up his. "I like this one."

His eyes lit with amusement. "You obviously know your reels."

I have four brothers and a dad who love to fish. Even if I didn't enjoy it, I would know reels. And this is a nice one."

"Then let's see what you can do."

"I'm not fishing alone. Let's see what we can all do."

Polly immediately put her line in the water. And immediately squealed in delight when a fish took her bait and ran with it.

And that was how the next hour went. One fish after the other and a lot of smiles between the three of them.

It was lovely. And Cassie hadn't had so much fun in forever.

* * *

Two hours after they'd started fishing, Hunter had relaxed and was feeling good. Fishing had always been his way to let the stress of the world disappear. And today he'd come out to the water, tied in knots inside with worry. But Polly wasn't bothered in the least about being on the water and was happy as a clam that he was with her.

They were headed back in and Polly sat with Cassie on the bench seat in the back as he headed back the direction they'd come. He smiled at his child and throttled down. "Are you ready to drive?"

"Yes, I'm ready." She started to spring up but Cassie held her.

"Wait until he slows the boat more."

He slowed more then held his hand out. "Now you can come over."

She crossed the two steps to him and he lifted her up into the bench seat of the twenty-eight-foot boat. "There's room for you, too, Cassie."

"Oh, good! I want to watch Polly drive." She came immediately and sat on the other side of Polly.

"This boat is different than the one we used before. I can barely reach the wheel."

"You're right about that. Here, let's do this." He picked her up, sat her on his leg and moved closer to the middle so she could reach the wheel better. That put his hip and thigh next to Cassie's. The day was getting better by the moment.

"I know it's been a couple of years, so can you remember what you used to do?"

Polly looked at him with big eyes. "I do. I hold it like this, and then with this hand, I grab this handle thing and I push it forward." She pushed the throttle hard before he could stop her and the boat roared forward, throwing them all back with the sudden force.

"Whoa." He held onto her tighter while he instantly grabbed the throttle with his free hand and eased it back under control. Polly was shaking. He looked down at her, and she'd gone white as a sheet. "Polly, what's wrong?"

Cassie looked worried. "Honey, it's okay. Your daddy got it under control."

Her shaking increased, so he quickly stopped the boat then turned her in his arms and hugged her to him. She buried her face in his neck. Her trembles radiated through him, hitting him in the heart. Her silent tears wet his shirt. "Pumpkin, you're safe. I've got you. Come on, tell me what's wrong."

"A big bird flew down and scared me." Polly's

words were muffled against his shirt, and her silent tears were now sobs.

Cassie looked confused and looked around; he suspected she was looking for the bird. It hit him then that Polly was remembering something that involved the accident, something that had been locked away in her memory. Carefully, he said, "The bird scared you but you're okay now."

"I screamed and fought it." She sobbed. "Mama let go of the wheel and turned around to make the bird get off me. She shooed it away but then the boat rocked, and Mama fell back on that handle thing and the boat jumped and went fast like it just did. I fell out of my seat it was so fast and I saw the rocks coming—then everything exploded and I woke up in the water." Tears streamed down her face and she looked up at him. "It was my fault, Daddy."

He closed his eyes and struggled to breathe. All this time, they'd wondered and couldn't understand what had happened to make an experienced boater like Sandra run full-speed into a jetty of rocks.

"Mama died because of me."

A tight knot that had been balled inside him eased as he finally got the picture of what had happened.

He wiped tears from Polly's pale face. "Pumpkin, it wasn't your fault. Your mother was one of the best boat drivers out there. But accidents happen to anyone. The bird was an accident. Your mom stumbling back was an accident. If the rocks hadn't been there, you both would have been fine."

"Your daddy is right, Polly. Sometimes accidents happen and everything is fine…and sometimes things go terribly wrong like it did for you and your mother. But it's not your fault and your mama would not want you thinking it was your fault."

Polly took a shaky breath, her eyes holding Cassie's comforting gaze. She held her arms out and Cassie took the girl into her lap.

The action touched the core of Hunter. "Here, let me help you carry her to the bench seat and you hold her while I get us home." Polly was little but she was too big for Cassie to carry. He held her while Cassie moved to the seat and then held her arms open. He kissed Polly's forehead. "You and Cassie snuggle while I drive this boat to shore. I love you, Polly. You remembered today and that's a good thing. Now you won't have to wonder what happened. You were right that we needed to come back to the water."

She nodded but didn't say anything.

He wanted to get her home and to take her to see Adam. After Cassie had her securely in her arms, he went back to the wheel and slowly, deliberately eased the boat back up to speed. With the wind buffeting the sound, he called Cassie's brother and told him what had happened. Adam told him to take her home and he would come by the house. It was a bonus having a doctor in the extended family because he really hadn't wanted to take her to the doctor's office. He wanted her at home where she could rest.

He glanced over his shoulder. Cassie had Polly enveloped in her arms and held her so tenderly as she rocked her and spoke softly to her. He owed her. His heart swelled with gratitude...and as she smiled that sense of connection strengthened.

CHAPTER NINE

Cassie waited in Hunter's kitchen for him and Adam to come out of Polly's room. She busied herself making coffee and setting out some cheese and crackers. She didn't think Hunter would be hungry, she wasn't, but it gave her something to do.

Today had drained them both. She prayed Polly was okay, that this was helpful to her in the big picture and she was finished harboring pain in the dark corners of her little heart. She had never experienced the level of emotion that had overtaken her in those moments of Polly's breakthrough or in the aftermath. She was still overwhelmed by what she felt, for the depth of emotion she felt for both Polly and Hunter. It was as if her heart was intertwined with them and she was a part of them.

But she wasn't. The reminder had been coming on a thirty-second loop calling out to her over and over again, trying to pull her back from the edge of letting her heart get too involved.

She paused in arranging the cheese on a plate when Adam and Hunter emerged from Polly's room. Hunter closed the door quietly and they came to the island.

"She's sleeping." Her brother came around and hugged her. "I hear you were wonderful with her all the way in from where the incident happened. Are you okay?" His serious eyes dug into hers, searching for the truth.

"I'm a little shaken by the experience, mostly worried for her and hoping this was a good step forward for her. Is it?"

Hunter stood at the island, looking a bit dazed himself. He nodded.

"It is," Adam agreed. "Now we know what we are dealing with. For a little kid to think she caused her mother's death is one thing. And I think there's some survivor's guilt there too. Her therapist will see her tomorrow, and I think they can start a new dialogue. You two can, too. Just continue to assure her everything is fine and that it wasn't her fault." He looked to Hunter. "You've got a strong little girl in there. She's going to be fine. Now, I'm going to get back to the house and check on Rosie. She's worried about Polly, too, and with the birth coming up anytime now, I don't want her getting herself worked up. She'll feel better knowing Polly is okay and that this is a positive forward step."

"Thanks for coming." Hunter came around the island where she and Adam were, and he gave Adam a quick hug.

Cassie's throat tightened, knowing just how much it meant to him for Adam to drop what he was doing and come see his child. Adam was like that, making house calls when needed. For a highly sought-after trauma doctor, her brother had turned into a wonderful small-town doctor. He loved it. And she was so excited to see him as a daddy soon.

"Love you." She hugged him. "Tell Rosie to take care of herself and to call if she needs anything."

"Will do."

Moments later, she and Hunter were alone and the room suddenly felt much smaller. She offered him the plate. "I wasn't sure if you needed something to eat."

"Thanks. Maybe later." He stared at her and then he opened his arms.

Cassie stepped into his arms as if it were the most natural action in the world. They tightened around her; he buried his face in her hair and she felt him tremble. Felt the thundering of his heart against her own thundering heart. Felt the emotions surging through them both.

"I was so scared for her." She closed her eyes, breathing him in and holding him tighter. Trying so hard to give him comfort, and feeling lost and completely blissful in his arms. Guilt niggled at her for feeling blissful in these circumstances, especially when she was trying so hard to stay neutral. But she knew that was no longer an option. She was involved wholeheartedly now. She was just going to have to think about that later. Right now, she had this reality and that was exactly where she was going to be focused. Hunter needed that.

She needed that.

"I would have lost it if you hadn't been there beside me. You were so sweet with her, and she told Adam that you helped her feel better."

"I'm so glad." Her words caught in her throat, cracking as they made it out. She took a deep breath. "It's a miracle she lived through the impact."

"Yes. It is. Come out here to the porch. I need to talk to you. I need you to understand more about what happened." He took her hand and led her out the back door onto the porch. He sat down on a swing and she sat beside him. He looked intense.

"What are you not telling me?" New worry hit her.

"Nothing about Polly." He let his thumb rub lightly over the back of her hand. "The night before the accident, Sandra told me she was leaving me for another man."

Shock shot through her. This was not what she had expected.

"Yeah, I was shocked too. And it cut me to my core. I knew we were having a few issues but I just didn't realize they weren't normal bumps married couples went through. She'd become distracted—I thought that was because her career was taking off. We were at a fundraiser dance and fought bitterly afterward. And that night, I slept in the guest bedroom. I went for a jog early the next morning to try to clear my head before we talked again. When I got home, she had taken Polly out on the boat on the family outing that I was supposed to have been on also. I assumed she would be back and we would talk, and I would do what I needed to do to try to save my marriage. But she never came home."

"I'm so sorry. I had no idea. Did Polly hear you fighting?"

"No, she had a play date with the little girl next door. We were not speaking to each other by the time I walked over and got Polly. It was late and she was half asleep when I carried her home and put her in her bed so we managed to hide our being upset with each other from her."

He had been through much more than she'd known. The weight on his shoulders was much heavier than she'd thought. "You've had a lot on you."

"Yeah, but Cassie…the police truly thought, after I told them about the fight, that Sandra might have wrecked the boat on purpose. The man she'd had the affair with told them she'd called him, highly upset, before leaving the house, and he'd told her not to go out on the boat in that state of mind. I didn't want to believe that she would have deliberately tried to harm herself and our daughter, but crazy things like that happen every day in the news. And I've been so angry at her. Even if she hadn't done it deliberately, she shouldn't have taken Polly out with her when she was so upset."

Cassie cupped a hand to his jaw. "You need to let all of that go. It wasn't your fault, either, if that is where you are going with this." So many emotions washed over her as he looked into her eyes and a need so strong to comfort him was all that mattered—in that instant her good sense left her. She leaned forward and kissed him. She hadn't meant to but her heart hurt for him. His arms went around her and he kissed her back, tenderly, and then with a sweeping need for her, as intense as what she was feeling for him.

Both of their emotions were raw as he finally pulled away and kissed her forehead before tucking her into the crook of his arm and leaning his head against hers. They sat there for the longest moments, swinging in slow motion as the afternoon breeze swirled around them.

Her phone rang, interrupting the moment, and she pulled it from her pocket. Dex's name came onto the screen. She had forgotten about dinner with Dex.

"Oh, I forgot I was having dinner with Dex. Just for old time's sake. I can cancel, if you need me. I'm sure he would understand."

He blinked, and his expression was unreadable, distant. "No, go. You have a life other than me and Polly. You've done more than enough." He stood and pulled her to stand with him. "Thank you. But we're fine."

She didn't want to leave. "I can cancel. Really."

"No, I think some time alone will be good. Thanks for listening to me."

"Thank you for trusting me with all the truth. I'll keep it close and not tell anyone."

"Thanks. I don't want Polly to ever hear those details. She doesn't need to know them."

"She won't hear it from me."

Moments later, after an awkward good-bye, she drove across town back home and in disbelief that she had kissed him. It had been wonderful and she should be flying high on how eagerly and deeply he had kissed her back. But she shouldn't have kissed him. What woman in her right mind kissed a man going through such a traumatic time in his life? He was worried about his daughter, for crying out loud.

What had she been thinking?

What kind of person was she? What was he thinking of her?

* * *

Hunter had revealed everything about his marriage collapse to Cassie. He'd needed her to know the truth—why? Because he had known that he had feelings for her that went deeper than her just being a friend who was helping out. And then, looking into her luminous eyes, he'd hesitated on kissing her, and been startled by her kiss. He'd had a little girl who had just gone through one of the most emotional episodes of her life, and he'd dove into kissing Cassie like a man clinging to a lifeline. He had soaked up her gentleness, the feel of her touch, the comfort of her lips with every barren wasteland of miserable romance-less corner of his soul. He'd been lost in those moments and alive and felt a hope...that he hadn't even known he'd been lacking until Cassie kissed him.

The text message from Dex to her had come just in time to yank him from the edge of making a huge mistake. Now was not the time for him to even think about himself.

Besides that, she had a date with another man. He

had no claim on Cassie, so it shouldn't bother him…and yet it did.

* * *

The restaurant was one of the nicer ones in Sunset Bay. It had a waterfront view, linen tablecloths, and soft music that went well with the dim lighting. It was meant for romance, and Cassie felt about as non-romantic as a woman could get.

They'd made small talk about her family, which had a lot going on in the last year and a half and had a lot to talk about. They talked about his family, which was smaller and had far less going on than hers. With all of her brothers and Erin having fallen in love, it had been a whirlwind eighteen months for the Sinclair clan. They'd talked about the Sunset Bay Regatta that her brothers had sailed in months ago, for the first time in a long time. And they filled in any gaps with talk about the weather. When they were nearly finished eating, Dex smiled at her, and, like she had all evening, she wished he was Hunter and that made her feel terrible because of it.

"I've been following your career," he said, at last bringing up the elephant in the room. "I get it now. You've done incredible things with your life. Things you couldn't have done if you'd stayed here in Sunset Bay."

She gave him a smile, trying for an engaging smile because she needed to be present in this moment, and yet her head and heart had been left with Hunter and Polly. "I...have enjoyed every moment of my life so far. Every job is an adventure and I work very hard to get the best, the most unique but heartfelt photo that I can get. I live for it."

He watched her with all of his attention but didn't say anything.

She continued, needing to fill the space of awkward silence. "I couldn't have done that here. But that doesn't mean I don't love it here. I just needed to spread my wings."

He looked down and then out toward the ocean. "I've been thinking lately about leaving Sunset Bay. I know I was always set on staying here, but, Cassie, I would leave for you. I should have been willing to do that years ago."

He was offering to go where she went. Her spirits sank. She'd hoped this was just a casual dinner of friends catching up with each other, but now it was what it was. She girded up her spine and let her compassion rule. "Dex, we were always friends. And I hope I can still call you my friend. But that's all we will ever be. I've never had romantic feelings for you. I tried. But it just wasn't there, and I think you need to come to terms with that and stop holding out for me." Enough was enough. For his own sake, he needed to stop waiting on her, and she needed to stop feeling guilty for not loving him that way.

She'd gotten to know Hunter better in a week and she knew with all of her heart that what she felt for him was life changing. She would never feel that for Dex. "You need to move on, and find the woman who will love you the way you deserve to be loved. She's out there. Maybe you've already met her and don't realize it. But I'm sorry, it's not me."

He inhaled slowly, his shoulders rising then falling

as he exhaled just as slowly. "I knew that." He gave a joyless smile. "I've made you uncomfortable and I'm sorry. I had to try one last time. You know, go all in."

She smiled at him and touched his arm and squeezed gently. "I get it." She pulled her hand away and reached for her water. There had been no tingles of awareness, no fireworks…nothing like what the simple touch of her hand to Hunter's would do to her. "I'm just being plainspoken because I want you to move forward."

"I am."

They left the restaurant moments later and he drove her back home. He walked her to her door and she gave him a quick hug. "Good luck, Dex. I wish you all the best."

He held her just a moment longer than necessary, as if acknowledging this was good-bye. Then he released her and stepped back. He started to go, then paused. "So, what about you and Hunter? Y'all looked pretty cozy this week at breakfast. I was envious of the way you looked at him. I knew then that I didn't stand a chance but I had to make one last stand."

How did she look at Hunter? "I was just there because of Polly."

His brows dipped and in the light of the porch light, his eyes drilled into hers. "Now who isn't being truthful? You have never had a poker face, Cassie." And then he turned, stepped off the porch, and strode to his truck.

She opened the door and went inside. Was it that evident to everyone that she was falling for Hunter and his precious Polly?

* * *

By the time she showed up at Hunter's for her next shift of work, she had almost talked herself back to sanity. Her life was uncertain right now; she was playing with the lives of two people who did not in any way need the uncertainty of a woman who could not figure out what she wanted out of life anymore.

Polly opened the door for her and jumped into her arms. "You're here. I've missed you."

"I've missed you, too." She hugged her tightly and

her heart turned over like a puppy needing a belly rub. She was helpless in the arms of this child.

"Polly—" Hunter came out of his room, tugging his shirt down over his incredible torso, and stopped short.

Her breath caught in her lungs and they stared at each other.

"Sorry, I didn't hear you come in." He tugged his shirt into place and moved to the kitchen. "Were your days off good?"

He seemed to have distanced himself also. It was for the best. "They were good. Thanks for texting me that Polly was doing well. I was worried about you." She looked at Polly, who had climbed up onto a barstool.

"I did good. Daddy took me to see Miss Sloan— she's the lady I talk to about everything. She's nice and she says things like 'And how does that make you feel?' I told her it made me feel bad. But she told me, like you and Daddy did, that it wasn't my fault."

"It sounds like she is a wise woman, because it wasn't your fault at all."

Hunter shifted from watching Polly to looking at her. "We're making progress. If you need me, you know where to find me. I've got a meeting, so I have to run. Thanks for watching my girl." He kissed Polly on top of the head. "Love you," he said and then headed for the door.

Cassie's heart squeezed tight and she tried not to be hurt, told herself again that it was for the best. They were both pulling back. It was as it should be.

The rest of the week was the same. They met him for breakfast but they both talked to Polly more than to each other. She told herself it was for the best. The three days passed quickly and by the time he came home, she had gotten the message loud and clear that she had made a mistake kissing him and putting that whole uncomfortable situation in the midst of what had been a good working relationship.

Not particularly happy with the situation, she had her bag by the door the morning he came home from his shift. She was having lunch with Brad's wife, Lulu, and didn't want to be late. That was her excuse, anyway. Lulu wouldn't have minded if she was late;

all she had to do was make a call.

But when he walked in the door, Polly had other ideas. "Daddy, can we take Aunt Cassie to lunch on the pier?"

"We—" Hunter looked from Polly to her, and she could see the dread in his eyes.

She saved him the trouble of saying no. "I'm sorry, Polly. Thanks, but I have a lunch date already." She met his gaze straight on, feeling highly irritated, and was pleased to see what she thought was shame or regret flicker across his face. She lifted her chin. "I'll see you in three days—unless you have other plans."

For a moment, he almost looked as if he might say he did have plans. "We'll see you in three days."

Anger and hurt battled within her. And humiliation. Why had she put herself out there and kissed him? "Bye, sweetie. Have a good time with your daddy."

"We will," Polly sighed heavily, openly showing her disappointment. "But I wish you were staying."

What could she say to that? "Maybe some other time. But right now, I'm going to be late so I'll see you in three days." Without looking at Hunter, Cassie walked out of the house, hoping he didn't follow her out.

He didn't.

* * *

She had a date. Hunter rubbed his temple, was she seeing Dex now since their date on Saturday night? Dex had been upbeat for the last few nights, and he assumed his date with Cassie had gone well. Truthfully, he felt a stab of jealousy every time he thought of the two of them together, but he was trying to ignore it. He was surprised Dex hadn't said something considering everyone seemed to know he had a thing for a very long time for Cassie.

He and Polly went to the pier for lunch by themselves. She enjoyed a little burger place next door to the ice cream parlor, and she usually talked him into an ice cream after lunch. They got their burgers and picked a table overlooking the water to eat. He picked her up and sat her on the stool, then sat beside her.

They watched the seagulls and the pelicans as they ate.

He wondered where Cassie was eating. He should have known it wouldn't be here if she knew he was going to be here. From the way he'd behaved all week, being so standoffish, he wouldn't be surprised if she avoided him at all cost. Not that he really wanted to see her and Dex together—

"Daddy, did you hear me?" Polly tugged on his sleeve.

"What? Sorry, pumpkin. I was thinking."

Her pixie face scrunched in consternation as she studied him. He had the urge to fidget, not sure what his little person was about to say, but certain something was coming.

"Were you wishing Aunt Cassie came with us and didn't go on her date?"

"Why would you ask that?"

"Why do you look like you ate a lemon?"

He laughed, knowing she was probably right. "Because your question startled me. No, I wasn't wishing Cassie was with us instead of her date."

"You should be, because I love her and I want

her."

He coughed. "You've only known her for about nine days. And you haven't been around her the entire nine days."

"What does that mean?"

"It means you haven't known her long enough to love her."

Polly's mouth fell open. "I have too! I love her. She is the nicest person I know, and she hugs me and reads to me and we play dolls together…she makes my heart happy when I see her. The same as it is when I see you."

His gut felt as though he'd just been kicked—the truth hurt because he realized that was the perfect way to describe how he felt when he was near her, too. He chose his words carefully. They were already dealing with her new memories and he didn't want to upset her in any way. "Polly, Cassie is only here for a short while. You understand that, don't you?"

"Yes. But she might get lonely without us, so I was thinking she might stay—at least sometimes."

It made sense. "I don't know. She might. But her

life is really busy."

"But don't busy people love people too?"

"Well, yes, I'm sure they do. She loves her family but she can't be here all the time."

"We are her family. You should ask her to stay."

He looked out over the water as the kiss they'd shared filled his mind and caused his pulse to race just thinking about it. She had a date, though. Even if he contemplated pushing for something more with her, she had a date.

But she wasn't married and she wasn't, as far as he knew, committed to anyone. And he'd pretty much ignored her all week.

Things were a mess.

* * *

"You like this guy." Lulu smiled at Cassie, and her pretty green eyes that looked so vivid against her tanned skin and golden-red hair sparkled with excitement.

"I do, Lu, but he's made it very clear that he's not

interested in marrying again. But despite that, what did I do but kissed the socks off him the other day. And now he's barely speaking to me. It's aggravating."

"I find the fact that you kissed him of great interest. At least you aren't hiding behind plants and watching him from afar like I did your brother. Poor Brad had me so mixed up with crazy emotions and he didn't have a clue. You, on the other hand, did what you do best—you went after what you wanted."

"But that's just it. I don't know what I want."

"Phooey. You do too. You just told me while we were eating that you had an accident that could have killed you and you are reevaluating your life."

"But I don't have a definite idea of what I want."

"You are lying to yourself. You know."

Was she lying to herself? She had told everything to Lulu because she was so frustrated, and Lulu happened to be here at the time it all spilled over. "But what if I'm wrong?"

"Girl, relax and let nature take its course. You are putting entirely too much pressure on yourself. Let this evolve naturally. For the first time in your life, sit back and just relax and spend time with that sweet girl for the next six days that you will be with her and see what happens. The fact that you have such a powerful attraction to him and Polly after such a short time might give you a hint as to how hard you're going to fall in the end."

That was scary. She didn't need to fall in any way, shape, or form again, because this time there might not be a ledge to break her fall. This time, she could fall completely in love with Hunter and he might not return her feelings. And that was the scariest thing she could think of happening. If she left it as it was now, her heart had protection.

CHAPTER TEN

"**L**ook, Aunt Cassie, a manatee! I love the cows of the sea!" Polly exclaimed, pointing at the huge, slow-moving manatee as it had just floated up to the surface and looked at them with its tiny eyes. "Do you know why they call them that?"

She smiled and let the girl have her fun. "You tell me." Cassie had been raised here, so of course she knew.

"Because they are vegetarians—that means they don't eat meat. They only eat plants, like cows do. And there may be more to it but that's what I know."

Cassie chuckled. "That's what it means. You are doing great. When I was a little girl, I thought it would be cool to put a saddle on one and ride it like a horse in the water. I thought it would be fun to do that to a whale, too, but they are too big."

Polly looked at her as if she had lost her mind. "You can't breathe under water."

"They come up for air."

"Oh, that's right. But since my aunt Summer told me we aren't supposed to touch them, they wouldn't let you put a saddle on them."

"Again, you are right. No saddle on a manatee."

"Why are you and my daddy hardly talking to each other?"

The question came out of the blue. Cassie had arrived that morning and just like the shift before, they talked to Polly and avoided as much between them as possible. She was kicking herself for letting the stiffness be between them, but he really didn't act as if it bothered him. And though she was thinking about what Lulu said, she wasn't sure—she hated not being sure.

"We talk."

Polly frowned, a half-moon frown. "Not like you did the first times you stayed with me. I told my daddy I wanted you to stay because I love you."

Cassie's heart stalled. "Oh, baby. I love you too."

"I told him the day you had a date and he said you might not stay. And that I didn't need to get my hopes up."

This child was just so plainspoken. "I wouldn't hurt you for the world. But I do have jobs all over the world that take me away a lot."

"But you could always come back."

She said it so simply. Was it that simple? And besides, she and Hunter hadn't even talked about their feelings about one amazing kiss, much less about a relationship.

"I could. You're right, and I do. That's why I'm here now. But you know what, I think it's time for us to head to Lulu's Pet Paradise and play with the puppies. What do you think?"

Polly's face lit up. "Puppies! Let's go. Maybe we can wash some of them for her. I did that once at an adoption day they had and it was so fun."

Cassie laughed. "I bet she has a dog or a puppy that needs a bath, so here we go."

The manatee had sunk back beneath the seawater and disappeared, so they headed for the car. And thankfully the subject was changed as Polly chattered about her love of all things involving puppies.

Cassie breathed a sigh of relief.

* * *

It was a bright and sunny afternoon as Hunter walked out of the fire station. He heard his daughter's laughter and looked across the street at the dog park. Polly and Cassie were there with Lulu and Polly was playing with several small dogs. His spirits lifted and he watched Polly enjoying herself like a happy child who hadn't been through what she'd been through. Her laughter was balm to his soul.

He crossed the road, watching them at the far side of the yard. Polly was scrambling around on the ground with two small terriers. She jumped up and giggled as she ran them back and forth and then went down on her knees, letting them jump and danced around her, yapping. It did his heart good to see her with such joy.

Cassie spotted him and he lifted a hand in hello; she did too. Longing shot through him. He wanted to talk to her. He'd been a jerk and he knew it. He opened the gate and walked into the park, closing the gate behind him. He strode with purpose across the grass. She watched him as he came toward her.

"Hey, you two. Y'all have found the perfect thing to make Polly happy. She's having a great time."

Cassie nodded. "Oh, yes, she is. She and Lulu are going to go inside in a few minutes and she's going to bathe several that Lulu has ready and she is going to be in heaven."

"Yes, she is," Lulu chimed in, looking from Cassie to him with speculation in her green eyes.

"Have you thought about getting her a dog?" Cassie asked.

"She definitely would like that. You've got a dog lover there." Lulu looked pleased.

"I've thought about it but I already have my hands full with my job and then having someone to help out with Polly. I thought adding a dog to the mix might be more than I could ask of someone. Summer wouldn't mind but the times when she's not there, like now, it might pose a problem. A little girl and a dog—y'all don't think that's too much to ask?"

"I wouldn't have minded. I don't have a dog but it's because my life would be harder to maneuver with one. I don't need to add carrying one through airports to my list of things to carry. I wouldn't have turned down helping you because of one though."

Lulu shook her red head vigorously. "She's loving those dogs and just so you know, Suzi-Q and Spaz are not the happiest dogs in the world. They're kind of grumpy, but not with Polly. The kid has a natural way with animals."

"She has a way with everyone," Cassie added, with deep affection ringing in her voice. "Including grouchy little dogs."

He studied her. He had missed her.

Lulu moved away to where Polly and the dogs

were, leaving them alone.

"Cassie, I'm sorry. I owe you an apology. I've been terrible not talking to you, basically ignoring you. I don't know what my problem is. Selfish, I guess."

She shook her head. Breathed in and out through her mouth. "It's not just you. I wasn't talking either. I really didn't know what to say. I felt awkward messing our friendly relationship up by kissing you like that. I shouldn't have done it."

The kiss—

"Daddy, look. Look. I love them." Polly was on the ground; the dogs stood on her stomach, and she was grinning and giggling.

He laughed. "Looks like they love you too."

Lulu picked up one of the tiny dogs. "You two stay and talk. We're going to go start bathing pups. It may take a while."

Polly jumped up. "I am ready." She picked up the other dog and snuggled her face in the animal's fur. Then, grinning, she went with Lulu.

They moved through the gate then across the empty street to Lulu's Pet Paradise. He and Cassie didn't say anything, just watched them go.

He turned to her after they had entered the building. "Cassie, you did surprise me with that kiss. But you didn't see me backing away, did you?"

"No, you didn't." Her eyes were shadowed, wary.

He hated he'd put distance between them. "You don't have anything to be sorry about. I enjoyed that kiss as much as you did—I'm assuming you enjoyed it. It felt like it to me."

"I did. But then I felt like a high school kid, with all the worry about how you might be upset about it and the way it put an awkwardness between us."

"I can assure you that you aren't a young high school kid and I'm not either. But our lives are complicated. I backed away. And then you had your dates with Dex. Is he going to get upset, seeing me over here talking to you?"

She looked confused. "Why would Dex get upset if I was talking to you? And what do you mean, with my dates with Dex? I went out with him one time."

He was confused now. "I thought you had another lunch date with him. He's been upbeat and I figured y'all were an item again."

Her eyes widened. "No, we're not. I told him that night that I had never felt that way about him, and we could never be more than friends because I just didn't have romantic feelings for him. I told him to move on. If he's smiling, it doesn't have anything to do with me."

He was an idiot. No wonder Dex wasn't talking about them. She had totally turned him down, yet he was smiling all the time. Matter of fact, he thought he'd heard someone say Dex had a date tonight. "So, you don't have a date with him tonight?"

Cassie laughed. "Nope, not me. Why?"

"I guess that's what assuming gets me. But you're still leaving soon and that's one of the things that worries me. What if I fell for someone and then she went back to her life, globetrotting around the world to exciting places? And here I am, here in this small town with an adorable little daughter…what would I do?"

"I know. I have that same worry. But, you know, that's my life. And it has always made dating hard. But, Hunter, I'm taking the advice of several smart people, and I believe you and I have a connection that is undeniable. And maybe it's not an everlasting one, and I worry that it could hurt Polly. But she's a very resilient girl, and even she was asking me why we aren't speaking to each other—in her own words. She told me she loves me. And I love her, and that makes it more complicated."

He just listened, taking it all in. "I get it. But, Cassie, you're right—we do have a special connection. I've never had it like this. I've been thinking about you all the time and I'm wondering if we are both so scared of what could happen, and trying to avoid any kind of pain, that we will regret not seeing where it could go."

They stood still and silent as everything around them seemed to hold its breath. Even the breeze seemed to have gone still.

"I agree. So, what do we do about that?"

"Well, I have tomorrow night off and if I were to get a babysitter, would you have dinner with me?"

Her face lifted in a smile. "Yes, I would like that."

His heart slammed in his chest and his smile burst across his face as he took her hand. "Then it's a date. I'll pick you up at six-thirty?"

"That's perfect. Are you sure you can find a babysitter? Polly could come with us."

He caressed her fingers, enjoying the feel of touching her. "No, this is for you and me. I can find a babysitter for a few hours. I've had a lot of offers. Lulu is one of them. We'll give Polly a break from the two of us."

He felt her hand tremble and knew his touch was affecting her as much as hers was affecting him. Her smile lifted slowly and he felt as though the sun shone brighter.

She inhaled and tilted her head engagingly. "Then I'll be ready."

"Great." He gently squeezed her hand. "I'll be there at six-thirty sharp." He let go of her hand and took a step back, holding her gaze. Then, he turned and strode across the dog park with a big, goofy grin on his face.

* * *

Cassie had changed clothes numerous times before deciding on what to wear for this date. She'd finally settled on a soft aqua jumpsuit with spaghetti straps and a pair of strappy sandals that would be easy to slip out of if she and Hunter ended up walking on the beach.

They'd talked small-talk until the waitress brought their coconut battered fried shrimp. Easy banter about some of her favorite places for taking photos. She knew they were just skimming and marking off time, but she didn't care. She was happy to be here with him. And so thrilled that he seemed just as happy to be with her also.

When her amazing fried shrimp was almost gone she decided to move to a more personal level. "You are more relaxed tonight. Is that because Polly has progressed more than you'd realized?"

He surveyed her with questioning eyes. "You're kidding, right?"

Confusion had her biting her lip as she tried to figure out what she would be kidding him about. "Okay, I give up. What would I be kidding about?"

His smile dazzled her as he leaned forward and slid his hand over hers. Shivers raced up her arm. "I'm relaxed because I'm with you. I relaxed after I realized

I hadn't completely goofed up by sliding off the deep end after you kissed me. I thought I'd given you a chance to get back with Dex and to be frank, I wanted to kick myself."

This was sweetness to her ears, she fought off a wave of emotion, blinking hard.

"Hey, are you crying?" Alarm rang in his voice and his expression mirrored it.

"It's okay, I'm really glad you asked me out."

His hand caressed hers. "I'm glad you kissed me. And I'm glad you are giving me another chance. Now, how do you feel about finishing this meal and going for a walk on the beach."

She fought the urge to jump from her seat and yank him out the door and down to the water's edge. "I'd love it."

Less than fifteen minutes later they left the restaurant hand in hand and took the path from the beachside parking lot and headed out onto the soft sandy beach. The sun's glow was turning the blue sky an amazing mixture of melon, gold and sapphire as they reached the water. For Cassie, everything about the moment felt perfect. Her heart thundered louder than the surf as he tugged her close and slipped an arm around her shoulders. She slid her arm around his waist and looked up at him.

"Cassie," he said her name, then dipped his head to hers, taking her lips in a kiss that was instantly passionate. His arms shifted around her and her every cell of her being reacted with matching passion. She could travel the world, experience the most exciting and beautiful locales and sites they had to offer but this...this moment, this feeling of his heart-beat merging with her heartbeat was the only thing she needed or wanted. This was where she was meant to be.

Here in the sanctuary of his arms with his passion flowing through her, making her feel like she was home at last. She could have stayed there forever.

He pulled away before she was ready and searched her gaze, his breath was ragged. "Cassie, I'm falling for you and I want to tell you that now, before I make the mistake of letting another old boyfriend come in and steal you away from me. Polly has already told me she loves you."

Cassie melted against him, either that or sliding to the ground in a puddle at his feet. "I love her too."

"And what about me?"

"I've fallen for you too."

He smiled then looked pensive. "I never thought I wanted to hear those words again. Because I never thought I could trust another woman. But Cassie, I do trust you and I want to figure out how to make this work after you go back to work. My brilliant daughter told me that's what families do."

She stilled in his arms. Families. "What are you saying?"

He cupped her face and went completely still as his complete focus drilled into her. "Cassie, I'm asking you to marry me."

Her mouth went dry. This was sudden, faster than she'd expected. She'd thought she'd have time to get her business figured out.

"Cassie, you look like you're ready to run far away."

"No, it's just I wasn't expecting you to ask me to

marry you so quickly."

"I see." He let her go and looked stricken.

She hated seeing that look in his eyes and in that moment everything clicked into place. "No, I don't think you do. I wasn't expecting you to ask me so quickly, but I can't think of anything better than to quickly become your wife. I love you. And I love Polly and I want you both, if you want me anywhere nearly as much as I want you two."

"Yes." He scooped her into his arms and spun her around and as the sun disappeared on the horizon, he kissed her again, long and deeply and it seemed in that moment in time between sunlight and moonlight that it was just the two of them on the brink of their new beginning. Standing there on the shores of her small hometown of Sunset Bay...the place she'd always believed didn't hold enough excitement for her and now, it held everything for her.

She was breathless as they both came up for air, staring into each other's eyes she felt blessed beyond measure.

"Polly told me that we are family and that we will be here when you come home from your jobs. And I'm here to add that she's right. I would never get in the way of what makes you happy. Your career is so important to you and I understand that—"

She placed a finger on his lips. "It is. But, I've been missing something. I've been taking photos of others happiest moments in their lives and deep inside I've been craving that and when I had my accident, I had a wakeup call…about what did I really want out of life? And since I've been home I've been a bit lost but so very, very quickly, because it was truly meant to be, I came to know that it's a life with you and Polly and hopefully some more children too that I crave. That I need and want with all my heart. I want to capture our happy moments now. And others happy moments on the side when I feel really drawn to a project. But I'm ready to make my home here with you and Polly. With my extended family surrounding us. This is what I was searching for…longing for, life with you. I've been longing for us, and now that I've found us, I'm never letting us go."

He held her close, his eyes bore into hers with all the love she could ever dream of and he smiled so very happy that warmth engulfed her.

"You, Cassie, are all I could ever want and I'm so glad you came into my life. Polly and I needed you more than you can ever know. I'm thankful you made the choice to walk into our lives. We are looking forward to what the future holds."

She leaned forward and kissed him. She would do this for the rest of her life. "Let's go get Polly and tell her our news," she whispered against his lips moments later.

He leaned his head back to grin at her, his eyes twinkled. "Let's do that…but first just one more kiss."

She chuckled. "I'm not sure I can stop with just one."

"You, my love, are talking my language. I messed up our first kiss but I'm planning on spending a lifetime making up for it."

She smiled against his lips loving her life…and capturing the moment in her mind's eye, knowing this was the beginning of a lifetime of happy moments in time that she would never take for granted or forget. This was the beginning of happily-ever-after and she was going to enjoy every second of it.

EPILOGUE

Polly was waiting up when they walked in the door of Lulu and Brad's home. Brad was on call, so she had insisted that Polly spend the evening keeping her company, and they'd been playing with puppies. Therefore, Lulu told them when she opened the door that Polly had been in heaven all evening.

Hunter took Cassie's hand as they entered the living room, feeling a bit anxious and excited at the same time to tell his daughter the news. It was sudden, though now felt right because he felt so complete. He'd been so concerned for Polly and now it was time to move forward. Her mother would live on in her heart, but Polly had shown him she was resilient and had room and a need for more love in her life. And so did he.

When she saw them, she jumped up from the couch, letting the two puppies she was cuddling slide to the cushions where they snuggled together in slumber. Her eyes were bright and he was certain that this excitement had made it impossible for Lulu to get her to go to sleep at all. Although it was only nine, making it just a bit past her bedtime.

"Daddy, Cassie! Did you have a good time? I did."

He scooped her up into his arms and wound his other arm around Cassie, tugging her close. "We did. And we have news for you."

Cassie met his gaze with eyes full of love.

"You're getting married and we're going to be a family," Polly rattled out with glee.

He and Cassie stared at her, both of them speechless.

"Yes," he said after a heartbeat. "How?"

She giggled. "I just know. I knew it all along."

"I love you," Cassie said, and her joyful laugh rang out as Polly launched herself at her with open arms wrapping around her neck and pulling her close.

Hunter's heart was full as he held the loves of his life in his arms.

Lulu rushed into the room with her phone against her ear. Her big green eyes were dancing and she was waving. "Okay, you beaming threesome—we've need to be on the curb now. Brad's on his way, we're meeting the family at the hospital. Rosie is in labor!"

"Awesome!" Polly squealed. "This is the best day ever!"

Hunter had to agree as they all rushed outside, talking over each other in their excitement. Cassie had already called her parents, who were expected back the next day, and as Brad drove his truck up to the curb and they all clamored inside, she was laughing as they all heard Maryetta squealing with joy through the phone. "My second grandchild!"

"Yes, Mom, you're about to have your second grandchild." She kissed the top of Polly's head.

It meant the world to him that with all the longing for a grandchild that Maryetta had been experiencing, that in this moment, she truly had claimed his child as hers too.

"Everyone buckled in?" Brad asked, and they all called out yes in unison. "Then hold on. Here we go."

"Mom, I have to go. Yes, I'll call you from the hospital. And Mom, just so you know your other little plan worked too. Hunter and I are getting married."

Everyone erupted in laughter as Maryetta's squeals of delight could be heard once more.

Polly looked up at him. "I like this, Daddy."

His heart was full. "Pumpkin, I do too."

Cassie held the phone a bit from her ear while her mother could be heard telling Leo the good news. Hunter held his hand out to her across Polly, who was sitting between them. Cassie slipped her free hand into his and smiled, and Polly laid hers over theirs and leaned her head against Cassie's arm and sighed with happiness.

Hunter's heart was full, in that moment as he felt Cassie's soft hand in his and heard his daughter's contentment. And just like that, all was right in his world.

Cassie was so happy that she couldn't even imagine her night getting any better than it already was, but the idea of Rosie and Adam welcoming their baby into the world on this very special night was like the icing of a cake for her...or a muffin.

Holding Hunter's hand, as he held Polly in his arms, they raced into the hospital behind Brad and Lulu. They were all grinning as they crowed into the elevator and headed to the second floor.

"Do you think she's already had the baby?" she asked Brad.

He looked at his phone. "I don't have another text yet, so not sure."

The doors opened and they bolted out into the hallway. Tate and Gigi were standing in the waiting room and rushed forward to greet them.

"Do we have a baby yet?" Lulu asked, beating her to the question.

"Not yet," Tate said. "But Adam is with her and we're just waiting."

"This is exciting." Polly grinned. "I've never seen a baby born."

Hunter laughed. "And you aren't going to see it born today, pumpkin. But you will see the baby as soon as possible after it's born."

"Okay. Is it a boy or a girl?"

"We don't know. It's going to be a surprise to all of us."

Tate looked at her and Hunter. "You two look really happy." He looked at their clasped hands.

Cassie blushed.

"They are getting married," Polly said. "Cassie is going to be my new mama."

Gigi clapped her hands. "I knew it. This is so awesome."

Cassie hugged her friend and then Tate. "Thank you. I am so happy."

"Welcome to the club." Tate winked. "You're going to love it. And you'll find a balance for your life and your work. It's doable."

Cassie smiled at Hunter. "I'm so happy, and we'll figure it all out."

Hunter kissed her cheek. "We'll figure it out together."

The doors opened and Adam came out, looking tired but ecstatic. Her heart was full seeing her quieter, serious brother looking so joyful. He'd been at a major crossroads himself when he'd come home to Sunset Bay, and very unexpectedly he and Rosie had fallen in love. And now, their love had come full circle as he looked around the room. She was giddy with excitement.

"It's a girl," he exclaimed, grinning from ear to ear. "She's beautiful and amazing and Rosie is doing great. So great."

"A girl," Polly squealed. "Can she come play?"

The room erupted with congratulations, and Adam took Polly into his arms. "As soon as she's able we will let her play with you. She's going to be so excited to meet you."

"Can I meet her now?"

"Soon, but right now she's with her mama. And I

need to go back too."

"Cassie is going to be my new mama."

Adam looked at Hunter and Cassie. Hunter had tugged her closer and she nodded at her brother. "It's true. We're getting married."

Adam looked really pleased. "I'm happy for you two, and I'm going to go in there and tell Rosie if that's okay. She's going to love this."

"Please tell her. And give her our love."

"I'll do that."

Cassie took Polly's hand. "Why don't you come with me and we will go down the hall and watch the babies in the nursery. They are always so cute."

Adam set her on the ground then gave Cassie a hug and whispered softly in her ear, "Love you, sis. I knew you were right for this family. You're going to be amazing."

She blinked back sudden tears. She knew that Adam understood everything Hunter and Polly had been through. She whispered, "That means so much to me. Because it just feels so right. Like it was meant to be."

"I know exactly how you feel." And then he walked back to the double doors and headed inside to his family.

Cassie sighed and looked at Hunter. "One day soon, I hope you'll be walking through those doors to see me and our baby."

"I can't wait." He kissed her, and Polly giggled and started chattering away about a new baby.

Brad grinned. "We are all going to make Mom really happy in the coming year, I'm thinking." He hugged Lulu close.

They all chuckled because they knew this was just the beginning of the coming generation of Sinclair babies who would be born here on this floor of the hospital. Today was a day of celebration and tomorrow it would be even bigger when Marryetta and Leo arrived along with Summer and Jonah, and Erin and Nash too.

They were all about to head down to watch for the nurses to bring the baby into the nursery when the elevator doors opened and Mami, Lila, Birdie and Doreen rushed out of it. They were all smiles.

"Do we have a baby yet?" they all asked at the same time.

Polly raced forward. "It's a girl. It's a girl just like me."

All of the ladies beamed and started talking at once.

Cassie watched with delight. This was what it meant to be from Sunset Bay. This was what it felt like to be a part of a community that cared. This was where she belonged.

Her fingers itched suddenly for her camera as she longed to capture the photos of all the joy on her family and friends' faces. She smiled...then bit back tears when she looked over at Hunter, as he was taking photos on his phone. Photos of her and her joyful moment.

"I'm so happy," she said.

"You make me happy." He pushed a button and snapped another photo of her then took her in his arms.

And she was home.

More Books by Debra Clopton

Sunset Bay Romance
Longing for Forever (Book 1)
Longing for a Hero (Book 2)
Longing for Love (Book 3)
Longing for Ever-After (Book 4)
Longing for You (Book 5)
Longing for Us (Book Six)

Texas Brides & Bachelors
Heart of a Cowboy (Book 1)
Trust of a Cowboy (Book 2)
True Love of a Cowboy (Book 3)

New Horizon Ranch Series
Her Texas Cowboy (Book 1)
Rafe (Book 2)
Chase (Book 3)
Ty (Book 4)
Dalton (Book 5)
Treb (Book 6)
Maddie's Secret Baby (Book 7)
Austin (Book 8)

Cowboys of Ransom Creek
Her Cowboy Hero (Book 1)
The Cowboy's Bride for Hire (Book 2)
Cooper: Charmed by the Cowboy (Book 3)
Shane: The Cowboy's Junk-Store Princess (Book 4)
Vance: Her Second-Chance Cowboy (Book 5)
Drake: The Cowboy and Maisy Love (Book 6)
Brice: Not Quite Looking for a Family (Book 7)

Turner Creek Ranch Series
Treasure Me, Cowboy (Book 1)
Rescue Me, Cowboy (Book 2)
Complete Me, Cowboy (Book 3)
Sweet Talk Me, Cowboy (Book 4)

Texas Matchmaker Series
Dream With Me, Cowboy (Book 1)
Be My Love, Cowboy (Book 2)
This Heart's Yours, Cowboy (Book 3)
Hold Me, Cowboy (Book 4)
Be Mine, Cowboy (Book 5)
Operation: Married by Christmas (Book 6)
Cherish Me, Cowboy (Book 7)
Surprise Me, Cowboy (Book 8)
Serenade Me, Cowboy (Book 9)
Return To Me, Cowboy (Book 10)
Love Me, Cowboy (Book 11)
Ride With Me, Cowboy (Book 12)
Dance With Me, Cowboy (Book 13)

Windswept Bay Series
From This Moment On (Book 1)
Somewhere With You (Book 2)
With This Kiss (Book 3)
Forever and For Always (Book 4)
Holding Out For Love (Book 5)
With This Ring (Book 6)
With This Promise (Book 7)
With This Pledge (Book 8)
With This Wish (Book 9)
With This Forever (Book 10)
With This Vow (Book 11)

About the Author

Bestselling author Debra Clopton has sold over 2.5 million books. Her book OPERATION: MARRIED BY CHRISTMAS has been optioned for an ABC Family Movie. Debra is known for her contemporary, western romances, Texas cowboys and feisty heroines. Sweet romance and humor are always intertwined to make readers smile. A sixth generation Texan she lives with her husband on a ranch deep in the heart of Texas. She loves being contacted by readers.

Visit Debra's website at www.debraclopton.com

Sign up for Debra's newsletter at
www.debraclopton.com/contest/

Check out her Facebook at
www.facebook.com/debra.clopton.5

Follow her on Twitter at @debraclopton

Contact her at debraclopton@ymail.com

If you enjoyed reading *Longing for Us* I would appreciate it if you would help others enjoy this book, too.

Recommend it. Please help other readers find this book by recommending it to friends, reader's groups and discussion boards.

Review it. Please tell other readers why you liked this book by reviewing it on the retail site you purchased it from or Goodreads. If you do write a review, please send an email to debraclopton@ymail.com so I can thank you with a personal email. Or visit me at: www.debraclopton.com.

Made in the USA
Monee, IL
29 September 2020

43578556R00115